For Mary, who read and reread
And for the Survivors
Thanks for everything

Books by Penny McCusker

HARLEQUIN AMERICAN ROMANCE
1063—MAD ABOUT MAX
1092—NOAH AND THE STORK

Don't miss any of our special offers. Write to us at the
following address for information on our newest releases.

Harlequin Reader Service
U.S.: 3010 Walden Ave., P.O. Box 1325, Buffalo, NY 14269
Canadian: P.O. Box 609, Fort Erie, Ont. L2A 5X3

"So why don't you practice psychiatry anymore?"

Ellie looked away, hating that Clary had caught her so off guard she had to hide the panic on her face. "Why does it concern you? You can't be questioning my credentials, because you've already checked me out."

"And that makes you angry."

"You had no business poking into my background." Ellie found herself shaking with rage. "Doc's word isn't good enough? Is that it?"

"You're his niece, and where blood is concerned judgment sometimes suffers."

"I came to this town to practice medicine, and to cover for my uncle."

That word stuck in Clary's mind. *Cover.* Ellie had come to Erskine to cover for Doc, but she was hiding something, as well, something about herself or her brother. He didn't know what, but he knew he didn't like mysteries.

Dear Reader,

My goal, as a writer of romances, is to create a compelling and well-developed hero and heroine. They need plenty of conflict, so that even though we know they're going to get together in the end, it doesn't feel like it at times. And I like to add enough fun so we can smile a bit along the way. Of course, there are secondary characters, a setting and all the things that create an interesting and three-dimensional backdrop to the story.

However, when I was writing *Mad About Max*, the first novel set in Erskine, Montana, a town full of eccentric, sometimes zany characters sprang up around Max and Sara—and frankly, tried to take over at times. And while I'd love to take credit for creating them, I have to admit that these folks just kind of clamored at the edges of my brain until I waved a white flag and let them out. I'm not sure what that says for my sanity, but I've really enjoyed the time I've spent in Erskine, so I'm grateful they let me come and play for a while.

Crazy for Ellie is the third and last story set there, and while I'll be sad to move on, I know I'm leaving the town in good hands. Sheriff Clarence Beeber will always be around to keep the townspeople safe, and Dr. Ellie Reed will be there to keep them healthy. Clary and Ellie have their personal issues, and they're not going to fall in love easily, of course, but I really hope you enjoy the ride—and thanks for coming along.

Penny McCusker

CRAZY FOR ELLIE

Penny McCusker

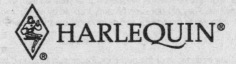

HARLEQUIN®

TORONTO • NEW YORK • LONDON
AMSTERDAM • PARIS • SYDNEY • HAMBURG
STOCKHOLM • ATHENS • TOKYO • MILAN • MADRID
PRAGUE • WARSAW • BUDAPEST • AUCKLAND

ISBN 0-373-75110-9

CRAZY FOR ELLIE

Copyright © 2006 by Penny McCusker.

Chapter One

If there was one thing Erskine, Montana, didn't need, it was another nutcase.

Deputy Sheriff Clarence Beeber took the turn into town so fast the big white Blazer that served as his squad car fishtailed, coming dangerously close to taking out the wooden Indian on the corner by the hardware store.

Less gossiping and more common sense they could use, but another crackpot?

He brought the SUV under control and shot through town at the reckless speed of thirty-five miles an hour, swerving around old Mr. Landry, who was crossing the street and took one hand off his walker long enough to shake a fist at him.

The problem was, Clary thought as he jammed the Blazer into an empty parking space along the boardwalk and slammed the door behind him, Erskine had a reputation. Most of the people here were a few personalities beyond normal, and every screwball in the state of Montana—not to mention Idaho, Wyoming, both the Dakotas and parts of Canada—figured there was a big old welcome mat at the edge of town for anyone who walked through life a bit to the crazy side of center.

He clattered up the steps and strode along the board-walk, berating himself with every ringing step. Aside from minor fender benders and the occasional citizen who left the Ersk Inn a bit worse for liquor, his town was clean. Clary intended it to stay that way.

"About time you got here," Dory Shasta said as he stomped by her.

"I was out at Ted Delancey's ranch, at the monthly meeting of the volunteer fire brigade..." He trailed off, re-alizing half the women in town were lined up along the boardwalk in front of the Five-And-Dime. Yeah, he thought with a mental eyeroll, why stay safely in your homes and businesses when there was a lunatic wander-ing around? "I got some calls about an itinerant loitering in this part of town, yelling at people and generally causing trouble."

Maisie Cunningham jerked a thumb at the Five-And-Dime's big front window. "He's in there."

Clary glanced in and saw someone hunched on a stool at the lunch counter to one side of the store. "Whatever's going on with this guy, having an audience won't help," he said, knowing it would fall on deaf ears and having to try, anyway. "You ladies go on home, now, and let me handle this, man to man."

"I don't think that's a man in there," Maisie observed. "I'm not sure what it is."

Clary took another look through the window, a closer look, cupping his hands around his face to cut the glare from the noon sun overhead. "You're right," he said, taking in the black T-shirt and black jeans, slung so low that most of the seat of a pair of black-and-white checked boxers was making an unwelcome appearance. His hair was black, too, and just brushed his shoulder blades, and even from where he stood, Clary could see the silver ring in his eyebrow. There'd be more piercings, he wagered, earrings, a nose stud, maybe his tongue. Clary had faced down armed assailants, and worse, drunk marines, but the thought of letting somebody pop a hole through his tongue—let alone the body parts some men pierced—made him shudder. He couldn't get a good look at the face, but only a teenager would willingly put himself through that; adults knew that living brought enough pain without self-infliction. "Not a man, at least not yet," he said. "Looks like a teenager to me."

"Who said he wasn't?" Maisie asked, looking at him as if he'd lost his marbles.

Yeah, *he* was the illogical one in town. "Mrs. Bessemer called and said he tried to steal her bags, and when she wouldn't give them up he swore at her and ran away screaming."

"Mrs. Bessemer is eighty-five. If he wanted her bags, he'd have them."

So why didn't he? Clary wondered. He crossed one arm over his chest, propped the other elbow on it and rubbed his chin, thinking about the three calls he'd had after Mrs. Bessemer's. Even the most creditable caller in the bunch had talked about the strange, crazy man in town. One call he might've dismissed as gossip-induced panic, but he couldn't ignore four eyewitness reports.

"He's only a kid, and a scrawny one at that," Maisie said.

"Whatever his age, I can't have him running through town terrorizing folks."

"He could have some sort of problem that won't be

helped by throwing him in jail," Mabel Erskine-Lippert, principal of Erskine Elementary and great granddaughter of the town's founding father, pointed out in her no-nonsense way.

"Arresting first and asking questions later don't seem right," Maisie agreed. "Maybe you should get some help."

The entire crowd of women surged forward, wide-eyed and eager, brains no doubt filling with outlandish suggestions. "Why don't you ask for Doc Tyler's help?"

Okay, not all their suggestions were outlandish. He couldn't pinpoint who that idea had come from, but it made sense to him. Clary didn't see any harm in getting a doctor's opinion. "Jenny," he said to the young woman who normally worked the Five-And-Dime lunch counter on school days, but appeared to have bolted at the sight of the lunatic in black. "Would you go down to the clinic and ask the new doctor to come down here?"

There was a collective gasp, and Clary knew immediately that he'd made a mistake. Erskinites took care of their own. The new doctor might be Doc Tyler's niece, but she'd only been in town a few days, and that made her an outsider. The doorway was blocked by several angry women, the rest of them gathering around him, a Prozac away from overthrowing law and order. Great. He'd gone from one peace-disturbing lunatic to a near riot, and there wasn't a heck of a lot he could do about it when all of the rioters were women who'd known him since birth.

"I know she's new in town," he said in a voice that climbed a couple of octaves in self-defense and a couple of decibels in volume to combat the angry rumblings, "but I understand she was a psychiatrist in Los Angeles. Seems to me she should know how to deal with this situation."

"Doc Tyler's the only doctor this town ever needed," Mrs. Tilford, the baker's wife, observed sourly.

That comment, of course, sparked off a heated debate, both factions trying to get Clary to weigh in on their side. Clary chose to stay out of the argument. Until they decided to settle their differences by taking a vote on how he should handle the situation.

"Don't recall ever doing my job by committee before," Clary said. "When did you all stop trusting me to make the best decisions for Erskine?"

There was a moment of silence, stunned, blessed silence he hadn't even begun to fully appreciate before it ended.

"Boy's wound up tighter than the playground swings at recess," Mabel said. "You need to get out more often, Clary, find yourself a willing gal and get those crankies worked out of you, if you get my drift."

He got her drift all right, not to mention a mean case of embarrassment that started at his toes and began climbing like prickly heat when the rest of his unwelcome audience joined in with helpful suggestions. He wanted to run, but he still had a teenager to deal with. And there was little or no chance of getting his audience to disperse. So all he could do was stand by the front door of the Five-And-Dime, gruesomely fascinated to hear women who'd changed his diapers, mothers of his school friends, teachers, librarians, even the school principal, talking about his sex life like a town full of Dr. Ruths. Take two blondes and call me in the morning.

"If you ask me he spends too much time alone in that vehicle of his, driving around looking for trouble," Dory said. "Erskine isn't going to have a crime wave if you take a day off, Clary."

"It sounds like you already have all the psychological help you need."

Now that was a new voice, Clary thought, momentarily forgetting about the crowd at his back and the strange kid inside the Five-And-Dime. Just the sound of that voice, slow and smoky and edged with sarcastic humor, made him feel as if he'd taken a fist to the gut. The sight of the woman it came from sent his blood pressure plummeting below his waist. He was a big man, a man who didn't mind it when a woman could look him in the eye. In fact, he preferred a woman he could put his arms around and feel as if he was holding something. This one barely came up to his shoulder and she had bones like a bird's. Eyes, too, for that matter—black and bright and lively. Clouds of ebony hair framed a heart-shaped face, delicate features and skin white as milk, even in the golden sunlight. He wasn't the type to let his imagination run rampant, but it took off so fast he didn't think there was any way to chase it down. And why would he when it was taking him places he hadn't been in a long, long, long—

"Elena Reed," she said. "You summoned me."

The dig didn't register, but the fact that she wore a white lab coat and carried a black medical bag seeped into the part of his brain that was still functioning and yelled *doctor.*

"You didn't call me down here to help dissect your love life," she prompted. "As interesting as it sounded."

The heat moving through him shot up into his face, reaching roughly the temperature of the sun. "I'm sorry for dragging you away from whatever you were doing, but it was necessary."

She smiled, a tight little smile with a ghost of arrogance around the edges of it, but it was enough to make him feel as if he'd taken a second punch to the gut.

"So what am I here for?"

She was angry. The snap of it was in her eyes and her voice, and although she delivered those words with cool, almost clinical detachment, they jolted him right out of staring mode. As she'd intended.

He hiked up his heavy police belt and folded his face into a frown. "I received four reports of a vagrant behaving strangely. When I got into town, I found him—" he gestured toward the Five-And-Dime "—so if you're done insulting me…"

She gave him a look that promised she wasn't anywhere near done insulting him, but she focused on the problem at hand by stepping up to the window. She took one peek inside, muttered a very undoctorlike curse, and bolted for the door.

Clary followed her, pausing briefly to glare a warning at the women trying to crowd in behind them. They lined up at the window instead, but it would only be a waste of time trying to get rid of them entirely when he knew they wouldn't go.

Once he got to the lunch counter, Dr. Ellie Reed, healer of bodies and minds, Hippocratic Oath-swearer, had the kid in black by the sleeve and was nose-to-nose with him. "Why aren't you in school?" she demanded.

So much for calling in a professional. "Maybe you should find out who he is and what's wrong with him before you scream in his face."

She rounded on Clary. "He's my brother and there's nothing wrong with him. At least not yet."

"Uh…maybe I should handle the interrogation." Clary pried her fingers loose and got between them.

"So why aren't you in school…"

"Luke," Ellie supplied.

"Shush," Clary said, and knew she was sputtering over being shushed. He had to work to keep the smile off his face. "I'd like an answer, Luke."

The kid scowled at his sister for a minute, then hunched back over the counter, worrying his thumbnail across a nick in the ancient linoleum and hiding behind a curtain of hair.

"And I expect you to look at me when you give it," Clary added. "A man faces his problems."

That did it. His head popped up, his eyes hot and resentful. "I don't have a problem. I didn't do anything wrong."

"Sure you did, but let's put the legalities away for a second and talk about why you're here."

Something flashed across his face, something surprised, grateful, and young and scared enough to have Clary softening toward him. He might be angry—troubled and misguided, certainly—but he was only a kid despite his efforts to put on a tough front.

Clary chose the stool opposite where Ellie Reed stood, purposely, so she'd be at Luke's back. He'd welcomed her help when he thought he was dealing with a lunatic; a normal teenager he could handle just fine on his own. And if it wouldn't help him to loom over the kid, he didn't want her doing it either. Petite or not, she had the moxy to loom. "It's a nice day," he said conversationally. "That why you ditched school?"

"I didn't ditch. I was sent home."

"What?" Ellie, voice strident, stepped to the side, facing them. "Why?"

Luke turned away from her, closing down again.

Clary looked at Ellie and shook his head. She backed off, but her expression went as sullen as her brother's.

"Let me guess, dress code violation?"

"What was your first clue?" Luke muttered.

Clary's eyes lifted to the silver eyebrow hoop. "Around here, the only male with a ring on his face has four legs and runs the open range with a herd of cows."

Luke's lips twitched.

"So, what kind of car do you drive?"

"I hitched back from Plains City, if that's what you're getting at." When Ellie sucked in a breath, he shot her a defiant look. "She won't let me drive to school, and I wasn't hanging around there taking sh— I wasn't waiting for the bus."

"You could've called me," Ellie said, her anger no match for the thought of him sitting in the front lobby of the school, taking garbage from the other kids. Poor Luke, not only was he the new kid, he was the new kid in trouble. But when she thought of what could've happened to him...

"He was probably lucky anyone came along at all," Clary said. "It's not exactly L.A. at rush hour around here."

She looked up and found him watching her. Ordinarily, she would've resented the fact that he'd read her mind and said what she needed to hear, but she was too busy being grateful that he'd put her fears to rest.

"So." Clary switched his attention to Luke. "Mrs. Bessemer says you tried to take her bags."

"I was trying to help her carry the dumb things. She's, like, a hundred years old, and, like, all bent over and stuff." Luke ducked his head again, clearly embarrassed by his own benevolence. "'Sides, if I wanted her bags, they'd be mine."

"That's pretty much what I figured," Clary said. "But she also told me you swore at her—"

"Jeez, what is this, Pleasantville? No piercings, no swearing. You people oughta be in black and white."

"Luke. Did you swear at her or didn't you?"

"I didn't swear at her. I just, like, swore. You know," he said, answering Ellie's question but keeping his gaze on the sheriff. Talking to him.

It stung. But at least he was talking. It was the first time since she'd told him they were leaving Los Angeles that he'd said more than two words in her presence.

"So you cussed," Clary said, "and Mrs. B. took offense to it."

"She asked me why I wasn't in school, and I said those assholes sent me home—" he flicked a glance at Ellie "—if you can call this dump home—because I wasn't dressed like a hick."

Clary smiled, damn him. He was supposed to take this seriously, and make Luke take it seriously.

"And the rest of the stuff you pulled?" the deputy sheriff asked. "Running through town screaming, for instance?"

"Everybody was, like, staring at me, you know, all freaked out."

"And you thought you'd give them something to talk about over pot roast tonight?"

He shrugged, but he was trying not to grin.

"So what were you doing walking down the middle of Main Street?"

"Trying to cross it," he deadpanned, his eyes going to Ellie's face, weighing her reaction again. "The traffic in this town is brutal."

"This is not a joke," she said, fed up with all the mental

back-slapping and bonding over stupidity that only men could understand.

"Now, Ellie—"

"Now, nothing." She dropped her medical bag on the floor so she could plant a finger in Clary's chest. "That's Dr. Reed to you."

"Here we go," Luke said.

"And that's enough out of you, Luke. You know the dangers of hitchhiking. If you're stranded somewhere—"

"There's no point in calling you because you're always too busy."

Clary got to his feet and maneuvered himself between the two of them. "Son," he began.

"I'm not your son."

"But I'm your sister," Ellie said.

"You're Dr. Reed. You said it yourself, and there's always someone else who needs you more than me."

Ellie let out a breath, stunned not by her brother's words but the bitterness in them. She was grateful that the middle-aged woman who was working the front register chose that moment to take Clary aside. He'd already shown how perceptive a man he was, and she didn't want him to see how much she was hurting. Somehow, that would make it worse.

When he returned, though, he paid no attention to her. "Mrs. O'Hara thinks she saw you put something in your pocket, Luke."

"That's not true." Luke turned on the woman. Just the way he looked at Mrs. O'Hara was enough to have her take a step back, one hand going to her throat.

"I saw what I saw," she said, her expression going sour at the notion of being called a liar by anyone, let alone a city kid who didn't have enough holes in his head already, he had to make more.

"Do us both a favor, Luke, and turn out your pockets."

"I'm not a thief." His gaze moved from his sister's face to Clary's, some of the defiance draining away. "I admitted everything else. Why would I lie about this?"

Ellie closed ranks with her brother, the two newcomers standing shoulder to shoulder against the Erskine establishment. For a second, Clary wished Babs O'Hara and her accusations to the devil.

"I'm sorry," he said. "I don't have a choice here, Luke, Dr. Reed."

Luke's hand crept toward his right pocket, and everyone's eyes dropped to see what he was going to produce. Then he bolted.

Mrs. O'Hara gave a little shriek and stumbled into a greeting card carousel, although Luke hadn't even touched her.

Clary whipped around to go after him, but his feet caught in Ellie's medical bag and he pitched forward. He reached out, strictly by reflex, his hands closing on something warm and solid. *Someone,* he realized—Ellie—but not quickly enough to keep from taking her down with him. His arms wrapped around her, and he twisted to keep his weight off her as he hit the floor. He lay there for a second, taking stock—until he noticed she was draped over him. He forgot about the aches and pains suddenly, lost track of cataloging the bruises he'd have tomorrow in the way her legs tangled with his, the wash of her breath on his neck and the softness of her hair against his cheek.

"I could use some help over here."

Clary ignored Mrs. O'Hara. In fact, the longer she stayed in a clinch with that wire rack the better.

"Dr. Reed," he said, sitting up and carefully cradling her in his lap. Her head nestled against his shoulder like they were a matched set. And wasn't *that* a dangerous thing to notice? "You okay?"

"I…had the…wind knocked out of me."

"What can I do?" he asked, instinctively rubbing her back.

"Stop that," she muttered, jerking her shoulders away from his hand.

"You're going to like it even less if Mrs. O'Hara gets an eyeful of you sitting on my lap."

She blinked at him, hoisting herself off his lap and levering herself to her feet. She stood there, bent over at the waist, dragging in air like an asthmatic, while Clary scrambled up.

"You keep breathing like that, you're going to hyperventilate," he said, reaching out to steady her—and deciding to scoop her up into his arms instead. In case she passed out.

He headed for the front of the store. To hell with Mrs. O'Hara's ongoing difference of opinion with the card rack. Ellie squirmed and demanded to be put down, but Clary forced his way through the crowd of women around the door and set off toward the clinic.

"Well, that's one way to get a woman," Dory Shasta observed, falling into step behind him.

"Yeah," Maisie Cunningham added on a hoot of laughter. "Next time try to catch one who wants to be caught."

Chapter Two

Ellie shut her eyes against the blinding white sun—not to mention the arresting male face that was way too close for comfort. It was a Superhero type of face, square-jawed, criminally handsome with warm blue eyes that peered worriedly down at her every few seconds. She put those eyes and the emotion in them out of her mind. It wasn't quite so easy to ignore the fact that she was cradled in his arms, that he was carrying her down the street for everyone in town to see. And gossip about.

"Put me down."

He only tightened his hold, practically carrying her pressed sideways against his chest, her face buried in the crook of his neck. He was so strong, so solid and homey-smelling. Each breath she drew was filled with the scent of him, starch, of course—his uniform had to be as stiff and unyielding as his personality—but then there was the smell of soap and sun-warmed skin that made her think of picnics by the lake, making love in the tall grass with a breeze caressing her bare skin—

He tripped, nearly launching her onto the boardwalk.

The tension that had started in her lower body moved up to her stomach. And not in a good way.

"Put me down," she gasped again, this time elbowing him in the stomach hard enough to make him grunt. But not cooperate. She grabbed his chin in her hand and brought his face down to hers, then blurted out the words "motion sickness."

Judging by the look of panic in his eyes, he understood, but instead of putting her down, he said, "We're here," whirled in a circle that had her head spinning counterclockwise to her pitching stomach, and walked backward through the clinic door.

Ellie got a three-sixty view of the waiting room, a blur of staring faces, as he spun her again. In the opposite direction. She planted both hands on his chest and pushed with all her might, catching him by surprise so that he dropped her legs to the floor, barely in time. She collapsed into one of the plastic waiting room chairs and went through the classic anti-vomit routine, head between her knees, eyes closed, breathing shallowly through her mouth.

"You okay, lady?"

Ellie lifted her head to see a little girl standing about six inches away, and when she didn't immediately lose the contents of her stomach, she sat up completely. And wished she hadn't. Everyone in the waiting room was staring at her, but that wasn't the reason she eased to her feet and inched toward the door leading to the examination rooms. Deputy Sheriff Beeber was the reason.

He stood by the reception desk, arms folded across his wide chest, a determined look on his face—as if he could appear anything but determined with that square jaw and perpetually stiff neck.

"What seems to be the problem out here?"

Clary swung around to face Doc Tyler, standing in the doorway that led to the examination rooms. "Dr. Reed was having trouble breathing." He reached for her, but she backed off before he could touch her.

"I only had the breath knocked out of me for a couple of minutes," she said. "I'm fine now."

"I think you should check her over, Doc."

"And I said it's not necessary."

Doc studied one face, then the other, but in the end caution won. He took Ellie by the arm and led her into an exam room.

The deputy sheriff followed, closing the door behind him and taking up a position in front of it, legs spread and arms crossed, a brick wall with a badge.

"Really, Uncle Don, I'm okay," Ellie insisted.

"Suppose you let me be the judge of that."

Doc Tyler had made the comment, but Ellie turned to the sheriff as the events of the last half hour came flooding back. "Luke? Where is he?"

"I have no idea," Clary said. "He took off while you and I were tangled up."

"Luke?" Doc Tyler said, laying his hand on her shoulder. "Ellie, what happened?"

She took a couple of deep breaths and launched into a rundown of Luke's latest troubles because she knew talking would steady her.

"Luke didn't steal anything," Doc Tyler said to the deputy sheriff as soon as Ellie finished. "He behaves badly sometimes, and he's difficult to reach, sullen, uncommunicative. After everything he's gone through, that's to be expected. But he's never done anything illegal."

"We won't know that for certain now," Clary said.

"*We* already know," Ellie said. "That's all that matters."

Too bad Luke wasn't around to hear her defend him so rabidly, Clary mused. Maybe he'd cut her a break. But that wasn't Clary's concern. The kid had been accused of committing a crime, and Clary couldn't say otherwise because Luke had bolted before he could get the truth out of him. "I ought to arrest you," he muttered to Ellie.

"What did I do?"

"Obstruction of justice. If I hadn't tripped over your medical bag, I might've caught up with Luke."

"I'm only sorry I didn't do it on purpose."

"If Mrs. O'Hara had watched him turn out his pockets we could've settled this thing one way or another."

"I wouldn't give that old battleaxe the satisfaction of watching you search my brother."

"No, now she'll only have the satisfaction of spreading it through town that he's a thief."

"Then maybe you should arrest her for slander."

"She thinks she's telling the truth, and I can't prove she's not because Luke doesn't have the sense to see I'm right and you're too stubborn to admit it."

"Stubborn!" Elle jerked up her chin to glare at him, the sudden movement sending a streak of pain through her head.

Clary didn't notice her wince, but Doc Tyler did. He nudged her into a chair, stepping between her and Clary. "If you children are through poking at each other, I'd like to look you over, Ellie."

"I'm fine. I've been fighting a stress headache the entire day, which isn't getting any better with this overgrown, arrogant rent-a-cop yelling at me."

"Rent-a-cop?"

"You seem so fond of adjectives," Ellie said sweetly. "I thought your limited vocabulary could use some help."

"I don't imagine it helps your headache to clench your teeth like that," Doc observed mildly. "Now settle down, Ellie, and let me take a look at you." He ran his fingers gently over her scalp. "No lumps, and nothing feels particularly sore."

"I didn't hit my head."

"I'm just covering all the bases. You said you were out of breath. Did you take a blow to the stomach or ribs?"

"Ask him, he tackled me."

"When I realized we were going down I kind of grabbed onto her so she wouldn't get hurt," Clary said.

"It was probably the combination of you squeezing too tightly and the impact with the floor," Doc said.

"She didn't hit the floor, she hit my chest."

"It must be made of granite," Ellie mumbled, "like your personality."

He held her gaze for a second, and she swore he was trying not to smile. "You wound up draped over me like a blanket, you know."

"And I was so anxious to get up, I stood too fast," she countered, ignoring the part of the memory that included being in his lap. "My blood pressure must've bottomed out."

"She nearly threw up," Clary reminded Doc, his eyes still on hers.

"I nearly threw up because I get motion sickness and Wyatt Earp over there wouldn't put me down. Examination over." She slipped around her uncle, but Wyatt wouldn't budge. "I'd like to leave."

"Not until Doc finishes looking you over."

Ellie sighed heavily. "Fine, but not with you in the room."

"Quite right." Doc unlooped his stethoscope from around his neck, inserting the earpieces and warming the bell between his hands. "I'm sure you have business elsewhere, Clary."

"I didn't see any stocks in the town square," Ellie threw in when it seemed as if he might hold his ground. "Why don't you trot off and build some?"

Dirty Clary, the Enforcer of Erskine, Montana, fixed one last disgruntled look at her and stomped off toward the waiting room, which was no doubt filled with enquiring minds. Ellie hadn't been in town long, but she already knew that the citizens of this town took their gossip seriously.

"What?" she said when she saw that Doc was frowning at her. "Are you going to tell me he doesn't have a puritanical sense of right and wrong?"

"If you ask me, more places in the world could do with Clary's brand of law enforcement. He may view the world in a black-and-white fashion, but he also bends over backward to be fair."

"I don't think he was very fair to Luke," she grumbled. But she had to admit it wasn't really unreasonable to ask Luke to turn out his pockets; Clary Beeber didn't know her brother like she did, and it would've been the easiest way to put the matter to rest. "Luke doesn't need any more trouble right now. He's confused and unhappy enough as it is."

"And you feel you're to blame for it."

"I am to blame for it." She chose a lollipop from the jar on the counter by the sink. Cherry was her favorite, but any flavor would've been an improvement over the sour taste in the back of her throat. "It was my decision to move here."

"Nonsense." Doc set his fingers on her wrist and consulted his watch. "There's more going on with Luke than moving here and you know it."

Yes, she did know. She'd lost her parents, too, hadn't she? Except she'd been twenty-three years old to his ten, she'd been starting her internship and able to lose herself in medical textbooks and round-the-clock shifts at the hospital. Luke had been shunted off to their grandmother's, and while they'd both loved the old woman dearly, she hadn't been in the best of health. He'd spent every day of his four years with her wondering if today was the day he'd lose her, too. Ellie hadn't realized until her grandmother's funeral, that her death had set Luke free in a way, that he was as relieved as he was bereaved. Even after a year he still felt guilty over that, Ellie knew he did, but she didn't know how to convince him it was perfectly normal, it was understandable and it was all right. And that was another example of how she'd failed him.

"That was quite the heavy sigh," Doc said, peering at her over the tops of his glasses.

"I'm sorry, Uncle Don. Nothing is working out as I'd hoped it would. I needed a change so badly, and I thought coming here would be good for Luke, but it's not, and now…"

Doc picked up a folder and took a pen from his pocket and scrawled a couple of lines. Ellie was thanking providence that he hadn't pushed her to finish that thought, and then he said, "Now what?"

"Well, for starters, the whole town knows I used to be a psychiatrist."

"Well, that's unfortunate, but maybe it's best that it's come out now. Some people might even choose to see you instead of me because of it."

Ellie paced across to the examination table and boosted herself up, then found she was too keyed up to sit. "I came here to practice medicine, not psychiatry."

"You're too talented a doctor to believe there isn't some of one in the other, Ellie."

"Absolutely, but what gives Deputy Sheriff Beeber the right to tell everyone about my personal business? I mean, I don't blame you for telling him, Uncle Don—"

"I didn't tell him."

That stopped her in her tracks. Her stomach gave a lurch. "How does he know, then?"

Her uncle shrugged and went back to his scribbling as if her world hadn't just taken an unsettling turn. "Why don't you ask him?"

"No! I…I'd rather that stay where I left it."

"You know better than that, Ellie. Your past doesn't haunt you because other people know about it." He scribbled a couple of sentences on a chart and set it on the counter, then looked up at her blandly, as if he hadn't cut her off at the knees.

Here she was, a psychiatrist trained by the best, someone skilled at cutting through the games a mind could play on its owner. Yet she'd almost convinced herself that if she ran far enough and fast enough, she could leave the pain, all that debilitating guilt, behind her. And with one pithy observation, an old country doctor made a mockery of both her professional knowledge and her confidence that she was a woman who always faced the truth.

"I'm sorry, Ellie. I shouldn't have said that, but I only want what's best for you. If my sister were alive—" he broke off, sniffing briskly.

"If Mom were alive, she'd be happy knowing we came to live with you."

"And you really should cut Clary a break," Doc continued. "He's almost surely blaming himself for the fact that you took ill."

"I'm not ill," she insisted, swatting at his hands when he came at her with the stethoscope.

He calmly evaded her attempts to fend him off and laid the bell on her back, moving it around a couple of times with the mild instruction to cough. "Well, your heartbeat's good and healthy, anyway. When did you last eat?"

"This morning. When did *you* last eat?" She took the stethoscope and urged him gently into a chair. "More importantly, when did you sleep? I bet it wasn't last night."

He was barely out of his fifties, but he looked older. A day's growth of gray-shot stubble did nothing to detract from the sallow cast to his skin, neither did his red-rimmed eyes. "At least your lungs are clear and your heartbeat is steady and strong."

She picked up an ophthalmoscope from the stainless steel counter against the wall and plucked the penlight from his shirt pocket, bending to peer into his eyes, first one then the other. "You're in pretty good shape for a guy who doesn't look so great, except you work too hard and fail to take care of yourself properly."

"Got all that from my heart and eyes, did you?"

"No, from the lines on your forehead."

Doc smiled. "Those are age lines, Ellie."

"Uh-huh. And what did you do last night? And don't even think of doctoring the facts. I only started seeing patients a few days ago, but I'm already plugged into the underground in this town."

"Then you know I drove over to Plains City last night to deliver a very beautiful, very healthy baby boy because his mother insisted on having him at home and there's no qualified midwife within a two-hundred mile radius."

"And this morning you did a circuit of the outlying ranches to check on an outbreak of chicken pox."

"Chicken pox is nothing to take lightly, but I'm happy to say the patients are coming along nicely."

"And you wouldn't dream of canceling your clinic hours, even with me here to take up some of the slack."

"The people here don't know you. The vast majority haven't met you yet, Ellie, and even after they do, it'll be awhile before they trust you."

And they wouldn't, Ellie understood, until she trusted herself again. "Trust takes time."

"For some people, that time never comes."

"Are you talking about the deputy sheriff?"

"Clary will come around, you'll see." Doc climbed stiffly to his feet. "There are those, Ellie, who don't like change. Some of them are old, and I'll continue to see them, since there's as much friendship as medical care going on there. But there are others who'll resist your help, and they're generally the kind of people who'll try to make it seem like your failing, rather than their own. Don't let them do that to you.

"Now take something for that headache, then go home, eat and get some rest."

"But—"

"I'll see you in the morning." And he was gone, probably straight to Maryann, the receptionist/nurse, with instructions that Dr. Reed was leaving. Even if she stuck around, there'd be no patients sent her way. Not that any of them were clamoring for her.

Ellie was determined to make it here, though, if only for her uncle's sake. As soon as he'd found out what had happened to her in Los Angeles, he'd asked her to come to Montana, then insisted, and when neither of those worked, he'd brought out the big guns, claiming he was getting too old to keep going at the pace a small, spread-out community demanded. She knew he'd overstated the facts, but what had come through loud and clear was his trust in her. More important, he trusted her with the lives of the patients in his care.

Ellie hoped she never let him—or any of them—down.

ELLIE MIGHT HAVE SUSPECTED Deputy Sheriff Beeber would be waiting for her. She wouldn't have expected she'd smile over it.

He sat in the waiting room, perched on a ridiculously small chair as all the big chairs were occupied. The same little girl who'd watched Ellie try not to vomit sat next to him, elbows propped on her knees, chin on her fists, staring unblinking at the side of his face. A bead of sweat trickled from his temple and meandered down his neck before soaking into the collar of his shirt.

Ellie slipped through the door and crossed the waiting room, knowing before she felt his presence behind her that he was going to follow.

"Allergic to bubblegum?" she asked as he fell into step with her.

"Huh?"

"Barbie-phobia?"

He snorted.

"You carry a gun, and you're afraid of a little girl."

"Damn straight," he said. "Little girls grow up into big girls and big girls become women."

"So?"

"You've met some of the women in this town. Don't I have reason to be afraid?"

He took her elbow to help her down the steps at the intersection and up to the boardwalk on the other side, and whatever response she might have made was incinerated in the jolt that buzzed through her, like a quick shot of electricity. He felt it, as well, judging from the way his fingers tightened before his hand fell back to his side.

By the time they reached the next cross street she'd braced herself, and if he felt anything, he was careful not to let it show.

"If you're talking about the ladies outside the Five-And-Dime this morning," she said, picking up the thread of the conversation, "they were only trying to get you married off. As persistent as they are, I'm surprised you managed to stay single this long."

"I didn't."

That brought her gaze up to his, and her surprise must have been answer enough.

"You've been in town, what, four days? I would've figured you'd heard everything about everybody by now."

"Some of the patients are reluctant to see me when Doc's available."

"They'll get over that. Or maybe I should say I believe you're too stubborn to give up until they do."

"I think there was a compliment in there somewhere."

He smiled, warm and wide. The sidewalk seemed to lurch under her feet, but they'd reached her car, thankfully, and she covered her sudden unsteadiness by stepping off the curb. "We were talking about you," she reminded him.

"I was married," he said, sobering. "My wife died while I was in the army, stationed in Afghanistan."

"I'm sorry." She laid her hand on his arm in a gesture of sympathy that was as instinctive as it was heartfelt.

He covered her hand with his large one. "It's been long enough that I've come to terms with it. But thank you for saying that."

"I should go." She pulled her hand free and reached for the handle of her car door.

Clary beat her to it. "I'm sorry we got off on the wrong foot."

Ellie avoided making eye contact with him; his body language told her more than she wanted to know. "I have a headache."

Clary started to smile, and then he realized she was telling the literal truth and not just reacting to the way he was behaving. But she could've been, and that was the biggest shock of all. He'd wanted her from the first second he saw her, but now that he'd faced it, he didn't like it any more than she did.

"I'd really like to go home."

"Are you sure you should drive yourself?"

She took a deep breath, and he had to respect the way she kept herself under control. She was a lot better at it than he was—something else to remember about her.

"I appreciate you walking me to my car, Deputy Sheriff, but I'm perfectly capable of taking it from here."

"Just doing my job, ma'am."

Ellie looked up, half expecting him to tug on the brim of his hat. Instead, her eyes collided with his and she forgot about the fact that she objected to being called ma'am in that slow, sarcastic drawl. Staring into his eyes, she could see he was much more complex than she'd expected, and frighteningly capable of inspiring in her emotions she had neither the desire to feel nor the strength to deal with.

Then the moment passed and they were sheriff and outsider again, and she convinced herself she'd only imagined…possibilities. "You don't strike me as a man who just does his job."

"What kind of man do I strike you as?"

"Someone who never takes off his uniform, even when you're wearing jeans."

"Pretty accurate," he said without an ounce of resentment. "For a woman who doesn't practice psychiatry anymore, you don't have a problem throwing your insights around."

She looked away, hating that he'd caught her so off-guard she had to hide the panic on her face. "I doubt there's anyone in this town who wouldn't agree with my insights about you."

"True. So why don't you practice psychiatry anymore?"

"Why does it concern you? You can't be questioning my credentials, because you've already checked me out."

"And that makes you angry."

"You had no business poking into my background."

"I didn't poke into your background. I made sure you have a license to practice medicine and that's it."

"Doc's word isn't good enough?"

"You're his niece, and where blood is concerned judgment sometimes suffers."

She had to give him points for that. She might be fuming, but she had to admit he went above and beyond when it came to looking after the people of Erskine. If more cities were as vigilant, fewer incompetents would be able to move from location to location, hurting people.

But then, mistakes weren't only made by doctors who shouldn't be practicing. "Uncle Don wouldn't put his patients at risk for anyone or anything."

She brushed his hand off the door handle, and he leaned against the side of the car instead. "Why is this such a problem for you?"

"Doc thought it would be best not to make it known that I used to practice psychiatry. He said it's hard enough to separate the real complaints from the mentally-induced ones in some people." Against her best instincts, she glanced up to see if he was buying her excuse.

He wasn't even looking at her, though, he was gazing out over the town. Humor lifted the corners of his mouth, the blue of his eyes warmed, and something inside Ellie yearned. There was such fondness on his face—the kind of fondness that went along with a shake of the head and a roll of the eyes, sure, but this was his place, these were his people, despite their foibles and eccentricities. He belonged.

She didn't. And he'd made it harder for her to. "I'd have been happy to answer your questions, Sheriff." Or evade them where necessary. "All you had to do was ask."

"If not for Luke, you'd never have known I checked up on you. And we would've gotten off to a friendlier start."

"I came to this town to practice medicine. And before you ask me why, my uncle isn't getting any younger. He can't continue to work at the pace he has been, every hour of the day and night, with no time off."

"And you came here to take over for him?"

"Do you see anyone else begging for the opportunity?"

"No. But I'm not sure you see this as an opportunity so much as a duty."

"He would never admit it, but he needs to slow down. He's the only family I have left besides Luke."

There was still anger in her eyes, but it was tempered now by love, and it caught Clary by surprise. He stared for a moment, felt things he shouldn't have been feeling before he pulled himself back from the brink of some foolish action. Like touching that soft white skin, cradling her cheek in his hand and kissing the sadness out of her.

She looked away, and he didn't have to guess what she'd seen in his expression, or ask himself if she welcomed it.

"He needs to cut his hours and he won't be able to do that unless the people in this town come to trust me."

"Which they won't do as long as they think you only came here for Doc and not for them."

She smiled that stiff, controlled little smile he'd come to hate.

"I've only been here a few days. Give me some time to fit in."

He looked her over from the top of her perfectly groomed head to the tip of her toes, clad in those fashionably pointy high heels he had no idea how women navigated in. Everything about her screamed *city,* from the designer clothing to the lift of her chin and the way she carried herself, as if there were a bubble around her labeled Dr. Reed's Personal Space. In a big, crowded city it was probably a necessary self-defense. In a small town like Erskine, people would see it as standoffish.

"I'm not going to change who I am or how I dress," she observed, reading his thoughts with the insight that seemed to come so easy to her. "Are the people here so shallow they'll believe I'm only what they see on the surface?"

"The people here are the most generous, friendly people anywhere. They're also small-town people who aren't used to a lot of change in their lives. It takes them a while to adjust."

"Well, since you're so good at disseminating information, you can let it be known that as soon as I'm up to speed, Uncle Don will be cutting back on his hours, and anyone who doesn't like it will have to deal with me."

Clary smiled; he couldn't help it. "I think maybe you'll fit in here, after all. Now you should go on home and eat and rest, like Doc said. Can't cover for him if you're not up to it."

He walked away, but that word stuck in his mind. Cover. She'd come to Erskine to cover for Doc; she'd convinced Clary of that. But she was hiding something else, as well, something about herself or her brother. He didn't know what, but he knew he didn't like mysteries.

Chapter Three

So he'd only verified her medical license. Ellie spooned up the last of her tomato soup and put it in her mouth, thinking *the big dumb ox.* What business of his was the rest of her life, anyway?

Hadn't he caused her enough trouble already? Broadcasting to half the town that she was a psychiatrist... Well, to be fair it hadn't been half the town. Just the ones who were sure to race home and jump on AT&T—Announce, Tattle and Tell. And then he'd challenged her to eat and rest, with her stomach tied in knots and her nerves still throbbing from everything that had happened. She'd had lunch because she was hungry, but she'd be damned if she'd go to bed like an obedient little girl....

And if she didn't she'd only be spiting herself, and it would still be a knee-jerk reaction to Deputy Sheriff Beeber's high-handedness.

Luke clattered through the screen door as she was washing her bowl and spoon. He stopped short in the kitchen doorway when he saw her. "What are you doing here?"

"I..." She stopped, deciding not to bring up what had happened after he'd raced out of the Five-And-Dime. He'd only blame himself, and the tension between them was already high. "I have a headache."

"This place is enough to give anybody a headache." He flopped down at the table, all arms and legs and bad mood. "I hate it here."

"We've only been here a few days. I wish you'd give it a chance."

"Like you gave L.A. a chance after that kid—"

"Don't!" She shut off the water and stood there for a second while the silence hummed with tension. "I couldn't stay there, after... After. And Uncle Don needs us."

"He needs you."

"Yeah, he's only interested in my help with the practice. That's why he's asked you to go fishing with him, and offered to help you find a car to fix up, and oh, about a dozen other things."

Luke shot her a look: defiance mixed, she was glad to see, with guilt. "I'm not his kid."

Ellie sighed. When their grandmother died, she'd made the mistake of thinking he was self-sufficient—and he was, when it came to school and getting his meals. But he couldn't feed his own emotional needs. She'd let him down there. She'd let them both down and now she didn't know how to reach him. You'd think, she mused sadly, that after training with the best psychiatrists in Los Angeles she'd know exactly how to fix this mess she'd gotten them both into, but when it was your own family, there was no such thing as clinical detachment.

Not that she'd been so great at that when strangers were involved, either.

"We have to talk about what happened today," she said. "I called the school."

"I told you what happened. If you don't believe me—"

"Will you listen a minute? I told them you're not cutting your hair, and if your idea of fashion is all black all the time, well, black's a color, too."

He stared at her as if he didn't know whether to cry or storm out of the room. When he dropped his eyes, she let out her pent-up breath. He was still ready to take off if she said the wrong thing, but for the moment he was listening.

"The boxers have to stay hidden, and you can't wear this." She reached up to teasingly flick his eyebrow ring, but he stepped away. "At least not to school."

She could see he was already thinking of ways around the rules. "This is the compromise, Luke, take it or leave it. If you leave it, you won't be allowed back in school, and there goes your future."

Ellie knew she had him there. He'd wanted to be a veterinarian since he was a little kid, and while his teachers might find him lacking in citizenship, academically he was always at the top of his class, his goal always in sight.

She ought to feel guilty about using his dreams to keep him in line, she supposed, but she didn't see it as manipulation. It was simply cold, hard fact. What she felt bad about was that he'd seen too much of the cold, hard side of reality for someone so young. "Things haven't been going your way lately, and I know some of that is my fault, but we came here for good reasons and we're staying here. Brood over it, go outside and kick the side of the barn if you have to, but you need to deal with it."

"Like a man?" he asked bitterly.

"Oh, Luke." *You're not a man,* she wanted to say, *you're a kid trying to cope with realities no kid should have to cope with.* But if she let him know how much she ached for him, he'd see her sympathy as pity and close himself off more. "I'm sure that's only one of the platitudes in Deputy Sheriff Beeber's handbook of 'How To Rehabilitate Criminals.'"

Luke snorted, smiling slightly and slouching against the wall. "I guess we need to talk about the shoplifting thing."

"I guess," Ellie said, although she'd intended to leave that for some other time, when her head and heart weren't both hurting.

"I don't steal."

"I know." She pulled out a chair and sat down. "But running made you look guilty."

Luke's hands went instinctively to his pockets, a gesture she might have wondered about if she weren't so tired. "I wasn't letting that guy search me."

"It would've solved the problem."

"If we weren't in this stupid town, it wouldn't be a problem."

Suddenly, it all seemed to crash in on her. Luke's unhappiness, her uncertainty over the move and the stress that came with each diagnosis she made. The next thing she knew she was crying. She tried to stop the tears, tried to keep her breathing slow and even, but it only came out as a sob.

Luke got up from the floor, fidgeted in place for a second, then settled for a couple of awkward pats to her shoulder.

"I'm sorry," she said, pausing to blow her nose. "You're my brother and you've had to leave everyone and everything you know behind, and I'm the one who's a basket case. I should be taking care of you—"

"I can take care of myself."

"I know, but… Can't we take care of each other? I know you're angry about being here, and I know you hate me for it, but I don't want to do this alone."

He dropped his head down so she couldn't see his face. "You won't have to do anything alone."

Her heart jumped into her throat.

"Didn't you see the way that sheriff guy was looking at you?" Luke asked, and the hope that he was ready to forgive her died. "He'll probably ask you out, you'll get involved with him and I'll be stuck in this time warp until I go to college."

Great, now he was angry with her over stuff she hadn't even done yet. But when she thought about it, she had to laugh. "You're already grumbling about the amount of time I spend working at the clinic and making rounds with Uncle Don, and you think I have time to date?"

The sound of a vehicle pulling into their driveway floated through the open screen door. "It's not what I think that counts," Luke said, glancing toward the window, then taking a step closer to get a better look. "It's what *he* thinks."

"Him?" Ellie whispered.

"Yeah." To Luke's credit, he went to the front door.

The sound of two male voices drifted back to Ellie, bringing her out of the surprise and then the reluctance that had glued her to her chair. She'd rather not see Clary at all, but she wasn't leaving Luke alone with him, and she didn't want him coming back to the kitchen like he was a welcome guest. Not after what he'd pulled on Luke. And on her.

"I always thought they should take out this wall," the deputy sheriff was saying when she entered the front room. "Completely open up the main floor of the house." He saw

Ellie and slipped his hat off. "I was telling Luke how much I like this old place."

"I'm partial to it myself," she said, and because her plans for it were very similar to what he'd described, she changed the subject. "Was there something you wanted?"

Clary looked from her to Luke, then back again. "I was hoping we could do this amicably but... We have to talk about what happened in town today. Reparation has to be made."

"What?" Ellie was outraged. Luke just rolled his eyes. "You can't punish him, that's for the court, and since he didn't do anything wrong—"

"I'm not going to arrest him, but he could do some community service."

"Like that'll happen," Luke muttered.

Clary went over to where Luke had braced a shoulder against the wall, his height alone enough to have the teen straightening. "This isn't Los Angeles, where the police don't have time to deal with petty offenses. I have the time and I deal with them."

"Yes," Ellie said, "why bother, say, a judge?"

"That's the way this town works, Dr. Reed." He turned back to her brother. "Look, son," he held up a hand, "Luke. By now everyone in town knows what you did today, and tomorrow it'll be all over school. Some of those kids will snub you for it, others will think you're cool."

"Cool," Luke repeated, shaking his head at what he'd consider ancient slang.

Clary steamrolled on. "Everyone will expect there to be some punishment, either from her—" he hooked a thumb in Ellie's direction "—or from me. Now, you paying a price for your misbehavior won't make any difference as far as the kids are concerned. The same ones who snubbed you will still snub you and the others will still think you're cool. But Dr. Reed will take some heat from the adults if you get off scott free. Whether or not you want to hear it, she's your guardian and it's her job to keep you in line."

"It's not her fault."

"I'm glad to hear you say it, but the truth is, it doesn't matter. If you're not punished, folks around here will know it and she'll hear about it. Since she's a doctor and bound to see a lot of people on a daily basis, she'll hear about it a lot. So will I."

"Because you're the big bad sheriff?"

"That's right," Clary said equably. "What you did might not be a crime, but you upset some people, and you caused some damage down at the Five-And-Dime. You need to step up and do what's right."

"Or you'll make me?"

"Nope. You say you didn't break the law, and I can't prove otherwise, so I can't make you do anything. But you looked me in the eye this afternoon and owned up to everything you did. Didn't deny it, didn't defend it, didn't whine or make excuses. Someone with that kind of courage wouldn't want to sit around knowing he'd made an eighty-five-year-old woman feel she isn't safe in town, or that he'd made a mess somebody else had to clean up."

"Like I'm going to go around town apologizing and stuff." He went red in the face just thinking about it. "What, is that supposed to make everybody like me?"

"It strikes me that a kid who'd own up to his mistakes would know it isn't humiliating to atone for them. It's the only way to earn respect, and whether or not people like you doesn't mean they can't respect you. And you can respect yourself."

Luke held his gaze for a second, his expression going stony, and then he walked away, through the house and out the back door.

Ellie felt tears threatening again, but she held them off. It took a mighty effort, and she had to turn around and walk into the kitchen to give herself time, but she'd be damned if she let Deputy Sheriff Beeber see her cry. She wasn't sure she'd be able to stop.

She went out onto the wide porch. Clary followed her, of course. Luke was gone; she hadn't really expected him to be hanging around. She leaned her hands on the railing, anyway, looking out over the place she'd fallen in love with the moment she'd seen it.

The land spread out behind the house and barn, easing into a little valley with a meandering stream at the bottom of it. Mostly it was a wilderness of grasses and wildflowers that waved and rippled in the wind, with a cottonwood or elm here and there to break up the flatness. An orchard took up about half the acreage, and rows of apple trees marched up the hill toward the house. From this distance, they resembled gnarled little gnomes. It was so calming—and hopeful, somehow, with the riot of new leaf buds forming a misty green cloud around each tree.

"I always thought it was a shame that none of the Mason kids wanted this place," Clary said from behind her. "You could make a tidy income with the orchard, and there's a lot you could do with the house. Like that kitchen. It always struck me as odd that a farmhouse would have such a small kitchen."

"You didn't come out here to talk about my kitchen,"

Ellie said, her peace destroyed by the deep timbre of his voice and her instant, breathless reaction to it. "If you're concerned about Luke 'stepping up' and 'being a man' you can stop worrying. If he doesn't do something, I will."

"It would be best if he did it himself."

She whipped around to face him. "I got that in the earlier lecture. And I don't need any advice about my house, so if there's nothing else—"

"You were supposed to be resting."

She stiffened, took a step back, away from the sudden warmth and concern she saw in his eyes. "I have company," she said, keeping her voice and expression cool enough to remind him the visit wasn't exactly a welcome one.

He took the hint, putting on his hat, and, to her relief, his dour and implacable deputy sheriff's expression. He lifted a hand and said, "I'll get out of your way."

Ellie could only hope he stayed out of her way, but he threw a glance over his shoulder as he walked off, and she got the sinking feeling she hadn't heard the last of Deputy Sheriff Beeber. Either professionally or personally.

Chapter Four

"Bessie's depressed, Dr. Ellie, I just know it. She's going to do something drastic if you don't help her."

"Bessie's a mule, Mr. O'Hara," Ellie said, somehow managing to keep a perfectly straight face. "What do you think she can do?"

"Well, she keeps running into the road and standing there." He leaned in and lowered his voice. "I think she's trying to end it all, if you know what I mean."

Ellie knew exactly what he meant, and suddenly it wasn't so funny anymore. "She's not trying to commit suicide, Mr. O'Hara. I don't think mules can formulate that kind of intent."

"Well, there's something wrong with her."

"Have you talked to the veterinarian?"

"Sam Tucker?" Mr. O'Hara snorted. "He'll only laugh at me, but I thought you being, y'know—"

"Yes, I know what you heard but even if I'd come here to practice psychiatry—which I didn't," Ellie said for the umpteenth time that morning, "I don't know anything about mules."

"Please, Dr. Ellie."

The look he sent her was so pathetic, and she was so tired… "Perhaps you should go home and examine where

Bessie is, um, housed. Maybe there's something about her barn, or whatever, that she doesn't like."

"I never thought of that." Mr. O'Hara jumped up, grabbed her hand and pumped it so enthusiastically he nearly pulled her off her feet.

As soon as he raced out of the exam room, Ellie dropped her head into her hands, closing her eyes for a few blessed moments. She wished she could've shut down her brain as easily, but if that had been possible, she'd have slept last night. Instead, she'd tossed and turned, fighting not to think about the deputy sheriff or worry about Luke. Trying not to dread her first solo day in the clinic without Doc there to back up her diagnoses.

Luke and Clary were still very much on her mind, but she shouldn't have given the clinic a second thought. The people who'd come to see her wanted her to fix their lives, not their bodies. And if they didn't want it for themselves, they wanted her to fix a husband or a child...or their mule.

"Dr. Reed?"

Ellie glanced up to see Maryann standing in the doorway, her pleasant face folded into lines of concern. "Who's next?"

"Nobody. I sent everyone home for lunch. There wasn't a real illness among the lot of them, anyway."

"This is thanks to Deputy Sheriff Beeber," Ellie muttered.

"Clary's a good man."

"If you like pigheaded, uncompromising—" not to mention unsettling "—men with tunnel-vision."

"If there's one thing you can say for Clary, it's that he makes an impression," Maryann said with a chuckle. "Now you go on and have lunch, Dr. Reed. You've only got a half hour before this waiting room fills up again. Maybe there'll be an actual medical problem for you to handle."

An actual medical problem, requiring an actual diagnosis. Just the idea of it tied Ellie's stomach in knots. This was supposed to be a new life for her, but how could she start a new life when she couldn't forget how her old life had ended?

For an instant she let despair weigh her down. It shouldn't be this hard. Erskine had all the makings of a fresh start: friendly people, family to help ease the way for her and Luke, even a man who seemed to be interested in her. Romantically interested. An attractive single man who, unlike the men she'd dated in Los Angeles, didn't seem to have any weird habits or fetishes. He didn't seem as if he'd resent her for making more money than he did, or get jealous because her job kept her away for long hours. No, he only had a very rigid sense of right and wrong. And she had a death on her conscience.

"Dr. Reed?" Maryann said gently.

Ellie glanced over her shoulder, mustering a smile. "It's a beautiful day," she said, letting the bright May sunshine lure her outside. Sure enough as she started walking her mood began to improve.

Even if Clary had been a different sort of man, she didn't have room in her life for that kind of complication. Not when she worked eighty hours a week and had a teenage brother who needed her—and regardless of what Luke thought, he did need her. In time, maybe he'd understand that when she decided to come to Erskine, she hadn't only been thinking of herself.

She'd honestly believed the move would be good for Luke. With their grandmother gone and her crazy work schedule, he'd spent so much time on his own. She'd been afraid his grief-driven acting out would only be aggravated by idleness and the opportunities a big city like Los

Angeles could offer a teenager with a self-destructive tendency.

She'd known it would be hard for him to leave his friends, but she'd hoped that being in the country might help make up for that. Luke could never get the experience with animals in the city that he could get in a farming and ranching community, and she'd believed there was nothing more important to him than being a veterinarian. That was another misjudgment on her part. There was a whole lot more to Luke than grief and ambition. She wanted badly to get to know her brother again. If only he'd talk to her.

As she walked by the diner, she was sidetracked by the scent of something that made her mouth water and her stomach growl. She'd planned to go home for lunch, but the tuna and crackers she had waiting there didn't sound so appetizing anymore. And who'd bother her in the diner? she asked herself. The way this town gossiped, people wouldn't chance having their personal problems overheard, right?

Wrong.

By the time she'd ordered the lunch special—chicken and dumplings—no less than a half-dozen people had come in with questions that started with "What would you do if," or "How would you handle," or, Ellie's personal favorite, "I have a friend." In Erskine everyone had a friend, but Ellie was rapidly making enemies. She trotted out some of the old standbys psychiatrists the world over used to fob off people who asked for instant advice—as though, because she had some letters after her name, she magically knew what was in someone's heart and mind without weeks or months of analysis. "Give it time," she told them, or "Go home and talk it over with your family." She got some disappointed looks, but no one pushed her for more.

Platitudes wouldn't put them off forever, though. Sooner or later they'd get comfortable with her and then she'd have to take a stand.

"Are you finished, Dr. Reed?"

"Yes," Ellie said, smiling at the waitress standing so patiently on the other side of the lunch counter.

She'd taken to avoiding eye contact so as not to encourage conversations. With this girl—Edie her name tag said—it wasn't a problem. Edie had the unfortunate habit of rolling her eyes back in her head before she spoke, as if she had to locate the words in her brain before she could route them to her mouth. Whatever she was trying to send down the verbal highway must've been pretty uncomfortable, because she stood there for a while, the empty plate in her hand and nothing coming out of her mouth.

If she needed that long to speak her mind, it was definitely something Ellie didn't want to hear. "Oh, look at the time," she said, glancing at her watch in case Edie noticed that her voice had risen to an I'm-not-very-good-at-lying falsetto. "I really need to get back to the clinic."

Edie's eyes rolled forward again, in time for Ellie to see the disappointment in them before Edie picked up her plate and took it to the busboy's tray. Ellie felt guilty, but she couldn't let it stop her. The man who was sitting next to her did, though, by placing a hand on her arm.

"Can I speak to you a minute, Doc?" he asked softly. The fact that he'd called her Doc, which implied acceptance, caught her, long enough for him to take her hesitation as agreement. "I could sure use some advice."

Ellie sank down onto her stool. "It might be better if you talked to the people who know you, Mr.—"

"Lem Darby."

"Mr. Darby."

"You can call me Lem, ma'am."

What was it with people in this town calling her ma'am? Ellie wondered. It made her feel about a million years old. But that was beside the point. "You should talk to your family, Lem."

"Got no family."

"Your friends, then."

"No friends to speak of. You see, Dr. Ellie, I have this problem and no one to bounce it off of."

Ellie didn't want to be the bouncee, but she could see Lem Darby wasn't going away.

"I don't feel like I belong in Erskine," he said, leaning forward so he could keep the conversation between the two of them. "I took a job right out of high school carrying the mail, thinking there might be some other opportunity for me here. Hoping…" He looked down at his square, capable hands and gave her the perfect opportunity to slip out.

Except now she wanted to hear the end of the story.

"Well, let's say I had my reasons for staying here, for taking a job I wouldn't mind working fifteen years later, if—if things were different." He heaved a sigh. "And now I've got so much time invested it's hard to walk away."

"It's a good job," she said quietly. "It must be something pretty important that makes you even think about quitting."

He shot Edie a look, and it all became clear. He was in love with Edie, but she barely gave him a second glance, and why would she? Lem wasn't unattractive, but unhappiness had stolen the spark from his eyes and made him look older than he was. Edie was a pretty young woman who probably didn't lack for male companionship and was used to being pursued. But a shy, unconfident guy like

Lem wasn't going to speak up first—or ever—unless he received some encouragement.

"Follow your heart, Lem," she said to him. It was another platitude, but in this case it was the right thing to say. "Only you can decide if it's right for you to leave town. Whether you stay or go, it's up to you to search inside yourself, discover where your path lies, and follow it."

Advice that she'd given herself not so long ago. Her path had brought her to this small western town, as much for her own sake as her uncle's and brother's. It was up to her to find a way to walk it in peace.

"I'd count it an honor if you'd let me escort you back to the clinic, Dr. Ellie," he said, adding a bit sheepishly, "there's another little problem I'd like to talk to you about."

Ellie tucked her tongue in her cheek and gave in to the inevitable. She couldn't avoid Lem without being rude, and honestly, he was such a sweet, mild-mannered guy there didn't seem to be any harm in listening to him.

CLARY'S OFFICE WAS a small room at the back of a larger room in the converted house that served as the sheriff's post in Erskine. The basement made a passable—if rarely occupied—jail; currently it was being used to store canned goods for the food drive being conducted by the Erskine Ladies' Charity, Harmony And Temperance Group, better known as the Ladies' CHAT Group.

Clary lived in the tiny loft apartment upstairs, and he wouldn't have had it any other way. He loved his job—he *was* his job, as a matter of fact. Erskine was his town; that was how he thought of it, His Town. He'd left it for a while, joined the marines right out of high school and become an MP so he could travel the world, but the world had held only sorrow for him, both in the service and out of it.

About halfway through his first tour of duty, he'd fallen in love with a shy, beautiful woman from a town near the base where he'd been stationed, and married her. Laura had never complained, not when money was tight, or he dragged her from base to base, or he was gone for weeks at a time. Even when his unit was activated, and he could see the fear in her eyes, she'd chosen to keep it to herself rather than burden him when he needed to be focused on his task.

He'd been in Afghanistan when he received word that Laura was ill. He'd been granted a hardship leave so he could be with her through the chemotherapy. When the time came to go back to his unit, he'd been torn between love and duty... He should have stayed with her, Clary thought, to hell with his duty. By the time he learned that the treatment hadn't worked, it had been too late for him to do anything but bury her. And duty was all he'd had left.

He'd lost his interest in the rest of the world after that. After his enlistment was up he'd come home to Erskine, and home was where he planned to stay. He considered the townspeople family members. And his job was to stand against any criminal or disruptive element that might have the poor judgment to impose itself on his family. It was as simple as right and wrong, black and white. And as far as shades of gray went, he was color-blind.

Or he had been until Dr. Reed came to town.

A week had passed since their meeting—or maybe *collision* was a better word. Either way, he couldn't stop thinking about her. And wondering. On the surface she was absolutely a model citizen: well-educated, well-behaved, what you see is what you get. And yet there were shades to her that puzzled him. She claimed she'd come to Erskine to help people, but when he'd called on her at the Five-And-Dime, she'd balked. Of course, he had blabbed to the whole town that she was a psychiatrist, and Doc Tyler was likely right about how that was going to play out. She had every right to be angry with him for that misstep, but that didn't explain the barrier she'd tossed up when it seemed they were veering toward a…less hostile relationship. Or the relief he'd seen in her eyes when he'd admitted he'd only verified her medical license.

She was hiding something, of that Clary was sure. The question was, did it concern him as a lawman, or just as a man?

There was no use denying the way he'd reacted to her. Thinking about it caused a heat wave inside him, reminding him that he wasn't quite as objective as he'd like to be when it came to Ellie Reed. And even if he hadn't been questioning that, the people in town already were.

The general consensus seemed to be that he should've arrested Luke on the spot, whether or not he had the evidence to support that action. Everyone thought the word of Babs O'Hara, a lifetime resident of Erskine, should be enough for him. As always, he'd used the law to defend his position—at least he hoped he had.

"Catching up on your reading?"

Clary snapped out of his thoughts to see Sam Tucker, the town veterinarian, standing in the office doorway. Sam had been his best friend since the first day of kindergarten, when they'd traded insults over who had gotten to the big slide first. After a halfhearted scuffle Sam had decided he really didn't care who won. Clary still maintained he had.

"Checking something in the county ordnances," Clary said. Whenever he could keep his mind on them.

"Heard you met the new doctor last week. I only caught a glimpse of her the other day, but I hear she's something—petite and slim with hair down to her waist and a figure—" Sam sketched an hourglass in the air and rolled his eyes in appreciation "—just the way I like 'em."

"You and every other man with a pulse." Clary slammed the Uniform Code of Justice down on the desk and sat forward, fixing his best friend with a glare. He'd been so wrapped up in his own reaction to Ellie Reed, he hadn't stopped to think about the rest of the male population. "She's bound to cause trouble."

"Sounds like the perfect woman for you, then. You're always looking for trouble."

"Not that kind."

Sam grabbed Clary's handcuffs, which had been sitting on the corner of his desk. "Any man who carries these around and can only think of one use for them is sadly out of touch with what's important."

"Ha, ha, ha."

"Jeez, lighten up. Do you realize how long it's been since a new, single woman has moved to Erskine? She's a breath of fresh air, and let me tell you I'm not the only man who wants to take a deep breath. Hell, Clary, you haven't had a date since…in a month of Sundays, just like the rest of the single men around here."

Clary knew what he'd been about to say, and why he'd changed his mind. Janey Walters had been the only single woman older than twenty and younger than fifty worth dating for miles around, and every single man in a fifty-mile radius had asked her out.

Clary had been in love with her.

None of the men had found their way into Janey's heart, let alone her bed, until Noah Bryant came back to town and reclaimed his high school sweetheart. When Janey married, she'd broken Clary's heart for the second time in his life. He didn't intend to repeat the experience. Ever.

"I'm too busy to date."

"Sell that to somebody who doesn't know you like I do. You didn't take your wedding ring off until you started sniffing around Janey, and you only dogged Janey because you knew she wasn't going to marry you. And now she's even safer—"

"Now she's married."

"My point exactly. Along comes a woman you're obviously attracted to and you won't do anything about it because you might have to take a risk, and if there's one thing you're not, Clary, it's a risk-taker."

"Yeah. That's why I'm in law enforcement."

Sam snorted. "Law enforcement is such a dangerous undertaking in a place like Erskine. You're a caretaker around here, Clary, that's all. The people of this town are the family you won't let yourself have."

Anger took Clary to his feet, but he held on to his composure. Sam was trying to get a rise out of him, but it didn't feel like their usual good-natured contention. "Where's this coming from, Sam?"

Sam shrugged, some of the bluster going out of him. "Neither of us is getting any younger, Clary. I don't know about you, but I've been alone long enough."

Clary felt such a deep and sudden loneliness it took everything he had not to let it show. "So stop notching your bedpost and get serious with some girl."

"It's not that simple," Sam said. "You know that better than me. You found the right woman once—"

"And I lost her."

"Yes, you did, and I can only imagine how hard that was."

No, Clary thought, he had no idea how hard it was to lose someone you loved more than your own life, let alone blame yourself for leaving her when she needed you most. It was the sort of thing that stayed with you for a lifetime.

"Maybe it's time you got back on the horse, Clary. Before somebody else—"

"Is that what this is about? You want to ask Ellie Reed out, be my guest. Hell, use my phone." Clary grabbed the ancient black instrument from its usual place and dropped it, bells jangling, on the desk in front of Sam. "You don't want the rest of the tomcats in this town to beat you."

"What are you getting mad at me for?"

"I'm not mad," Clary said, and forced it to be the truth before he had to wonder what being mad about someone dating Ellie Reed might mean.

"'Sides, I couldn't ask her out if I wanted to," Sam went on. "Doc Tyler has asked me to take on a trainee for the summer."

"Who?"

"Don't know. I ran into Doc out at the Lawsons' farm. The Lawson kids had chicken pox, and I was treating a calf that had a run-in with a barbed wire fence. Damn thing was bawling so loud I only caught every other word."

"Won't another pair of hands save you some time?"

"Had an intern once. Takes longer to explain something than to do it myself, not to mention the endless questions. Between that and the new breeding program on my ranch, I'll be lucky if I have enough time to talk to myself, never mind anybody else."

"Too bad I can't find something to keep the rest of the town that busy." Clary rubbed a hand over his face. "Maybe I should tell everyone to leave the new doctor alone until she has time to settle in."

"Do you really think that'll work?"

"If the people of this town listened to me a little more often, there'd be a lot less trouble."

"Because you know what's best for everyone? When are you going to figure out you're not everybody's father, Clary? You're the sheriff, and the last time I checked it was job, not a mission."

"You're lucky I don't toss you out of here on your ass."

"You could try."

It was a tribute to the depth of their friendship that Clary didn't. It took him a moment to work through his anger, but he finally admitted that someone as easygoing as Sam wouldn't have said something so inflammatory unless it needed saying. "I know I take my job too seriously at times, but somebody has to take things seriously here."

"You're going to serious yourself right into a heart attack if you're not careful."

Clary shrugged off the possibility. "I have to die of something and it's not likely there'll be a line-of-duty incident in this town."

"I wouldn't be too sure of that," Sam said grinning. "Half the people in your constituency have been to see the new psychiatrist."

Clary swore under his breath.

"You're the one who let the cat out of the bag. You know this town as well as anyone. It's only a matter of time before it backfires on you."

"And of course there's a pool down at the Ersk Inn."

The people of Erskine didn't just gossip, they liked to bet, too. Being a practical group, they'd found it only natural to combine the two pastimes and bet on the outcome of the happenings in town. And since a lot of the talking and wagering were carried out over a beer and burger at the Ersk Inn, Mike Shasta, the owner of the Inn, had decided to prevent disagreements—and possible damage to his place—by tracking the pools. Big white posterboards hung on the wall beside the door, and for five dollars you could mark your name in one of the gridded squares and maybe earn a nice little windfall.

"Of course there's a pool." Sam consulted his watch. "Seven forty-five. Looks like I'm out of the running— unless something happens in the next fifteen minutes."

"One of these days I'm going to shut down that damn betting wall," Clary said, although both he and Sam knew he never would. Technically the betting wall was an illegal gambling operation, but Clary had come to the same conclusion Mike had; shutting it down would only drive it underground and result in more bother than it was worth.

"Killjoy," Sam said. He turned toward the door, then back. "You're going to ask her out, right?"

"Wrong." But Clary wanted to, and that was the problem. He could still remember the feel of her nestled against his chest, the scent of her hair, the way she'd smiled up at him and made him want...

And therein lay the real trouble. She'd made him want things he'd promised himself he'd never want again— especially not with a woman who, with one look, could spark a conflagration in him that threatened to consume duty and common sense. And what would he be left with then?

"You have to move on sometime, Clary."

"Right now I'll settle for kicking you out of my office." He retrieved the Uniform Code Of Justice from the desk and picked up where he'd left off.

Sam hung the handcuffs over the spine of the book. "Sure would be a shame if you missed out on a future because of the past."

"Go away, Sam."

"Fine. Stay in your rut."

"I like my rut." But Clary found himself staring at the handcuffs. He'd always been a strait-laced, missionary-position kind of guy, but there was something about Ellie Reed, something different, exotic, that naturally led a man's mind, not to mention his libido—

The outer door slammed open.

"You'd better come quick, Sheriff," a breathless voice called out from the main part of the office. "You'll never believe what Lem Darby is up to."

Chapter Five

Clary grabbed his handcuffs—not that he'd need them, but they were part of the uniform—and bolted out the door of the Sheriff's office on Sam's heels.

"Hurry!" Owen Keller collapsed against a post to catch his breath as they passed him by. "Lem Darby is destroying my place."

Owen owned the market in town, apparently not a job that promoted good physical fitness. Or patience, or charity, or open-mindedness, or any one of a dozen other favorable human traits. In fact, Owen Keller was generally acknowledged to be a putz who charged the highest prices possible simply because he could get away with it, seeing as his was the only grocery store for fifty miles around.

He was, however, a citizen and business owner in Clary's town. The rest went without saying.

"Let me by," Clary shouted. "We're not in kindergarten and this isn't some stupid slide."

"Like hell." Sam deliberately took up the whole boardwalk.

Clary tried to shoulder him aside and Sam shoved back. The two of them jostled for position, Sam in danger of being slammed against the wall and Clary of being shoved off the boardwalk.

They rounded the next corner and nearly bowled over old Mr. Landry, who'd been heading toward them. Sam jerked to a stop, slapping both hands down on Mr. Landry's walker and ending up nose to shiny pink scalp with the old man. It was that or take him down. Clary jumped sideways off the boardwalk, raced around the obstruction, and leaped back up without losing momentum. Sam followed a heartbeat behind, yelling out an apology.

Mr. Landry didn't waste time shaking a fist at either of them. He whipped around in a circle and stomped off behind Clary and Sam as fast as he could, cursing the walker the whole way. He used words even Clary had never heard before, and nobody swore like a drunk marine.

But then, nobody held a riot like Erskine.

A crowd had gathered in front of Keller's Market, bringing traffic to a screeching halt—or maybe traffic had stopped itself, since most of the stationary cars had at least the driver's door hanging open and no visible signs of life inside. For a moment, Clary wondered why everyone was standing in the street instead of trying to peer into the store. Then something sailed through one of the windows lining the front of Keller's and hit the sidewalk in a shower of glass and a choking white cloud.

"Baby powder!" Owen Keller yelled as he arrived on the scene beet-red in the face, half bent over, huffing and puffing to catch his breath. "Damn fool must be in the baby aisle."

Sure enough, jars of baby food burst rapidfire through the window. Some broke on the boardwalk, but as Lem found a rhythm, they began to reach to the front edges of the crowd.

It wasn't enough to prompt anyone to go home, however. That would have been too much to hope for.

"Lem!" Clary took up a post at the edge of the first window where he would be safe from death by strained peas. "Come on out of there before someone gets hurt."

"I ain't coming out."

This was followed by another shower of glass that produced a two-liter bottle of soda. The plastic bottle bounced harmlessly on the boardwalk a couple of times before launching itself into the arms of one of the onlookers—who held it up in the air, dancing and whooping like a lunatic.

Great. Prizes. Now the crowd would never disperse. "I'm deputizing you," Clary said to Sam. "Crowd control. Make sure nobody gets trampled. And clear the street."

"How about I find the cure for cancer while I'm at it?"

Clary ignored him, turning to where Owen Keller was wringing his hands and staring at the front of the store. "Why don't you tell me how this started."

"Two broken windows," Owen moaned, "and who knows how much stock's been ruined inside. You have to get him out of there before he bankrupts me."

"If I go in there and try to drag him out, it'll only make matters worse." And not just to Owen's stock. Lem was in a rage; he'd be throwing fists if Clary busted in on him. Clary didn't want to have to hit back. Or worse. "I'd rather try to talk him out of there first. Why don't you tell me how he got in and why he's going crazy."

Owen tore his eyes off the front of his store, where muffled crashes could still be heard from inside. "I closed up at seven-thirty, like always. I was halfway home when I remembered Alva had asked me to fetch her a can of tomato paste for some Italian dish she's making for supper tomorrow." He pronounced it "eye-talian," fixing Clary with a sheepish look as he patted his ample stomach. "You know how Alva's always experimenting with the fancy recipes she sees on those cable cooking shows, Clary, and I don't object. But Italian never sits well with me, so I almost didn't come back—"

"Owen."

"Oh, right. Anyway, when I got back here, the front door was unlocked. I know I locked it because I distinctly remember—" The sound Clary made had him sidling a step or two away, but it brought him back to the subject. "Lem must have picked the lock—he can, y'know. His father was a locksmith."

"So you got back here and found the door unlocked. You went in and Lem was there."

"Cleaning out the cash register," Owen finished indignantly. "I only leave enough change to start the next day with—about fifty dollars or so. I don't mind him pocketing a tube of toothpaste now and again, but really, Clary, I have to draw the line at outright robbery. I mean, it's not like he's destitute or anything."

Lem Darby was Erskine's one and only postman and its resident criminal—petty criminal, to be sure, who pilfered from orchards and tucked the odd item away in his coat pocket when he was shopping. It wasn't that his job delivering mail to the outlying ranches and farms paid poorly, but that he couldn't seem to help himself.

Every now and then one of the shopkeepers in town called Clary when Lem got too ambitious in his thievery, but as long as the stolen items were returned, the matter would be dropped. Nobody wanted to go to the trouble of a formal charge, especially when Lem was such a likeable guy. Instead, the shopkeepers had taken to adding a dollar or two to his bill whenever he graced their establishments.

Clary didn't think a couple of bucks was going to suffice this time.

"The minute he saw me, he barricaded himself behind the counter and began throwing stuff at me." Owen indicated a darkening bruise on the side of his jaw. "Took a can of Red Man here, and then he threw a bunch of candy bars at my back. By the time I made it out the front door, he'd chucked most of the counter displays at me and was starting on the magazine racks. He locked the door behind me, so I hightailed it down to your office."

A bag of charcoal came sailing out the next window and thudded on the boardwalk, followed by a container of lighter fluid—Lem's two cents, apparently.

"He's going to light the store on fire!" Owen shrieked, grabbing Clary's sleeve. "Shoot him!"

"He's not going to light the store on fire. Are you, Lem?"

"I might if you don't get that greedy little pip-squeak out of here."

"I'm not shooting him," Clary said before Owen could bring it up again.

"It's not my fault," Lem yelled. "I've got an illness." He punctuated his statement with a wide assortment of items from the drug aisle—cold and indigestion remedies, feminine hygiene products, bottles of castor oil. No cures for kleptomania, but at least he wasn't letting his anger fester. "Dr. Ellie told me so."

"Yes!" came a shout from the street.

Clary looked over his shoulder to see Sam Tucker's fist shoot into the air.

When he saw Clary glaring at him, Sam shrugged. "I won the pool."

A bottle of cough syrup exploding on the boardwalk brought everyone's attention back to the store. Several more bottles followed the first, leaving sticky red puddles wherever they broke.

"He's ruining me!" Owen whined. "I can't afford to replace this stuff."

"Maybe you can get a loan from Sam." Clary hunkered down to retrieve the baby powder, which he poured on the castor oil. Then he snagged a bottle of aspirin and downed three. "Go back with the rest of the crowd, Owen, and let me deal with this."

Clary handed him the bottle of aspirin—rather forcibly. That, coupled with the look he gave Owen, was enough to send him on his way. "Lem," he yelled, "either you come out or I'm coming in."

Lem's reply was firing produce through the last unbroken windowpane. Heads of lettuce and baby carrots rained onto the boardwalk, followed by a smorgasbord of fruit— bananas, strawberries, grapes, even a cantaloupe or two.

"The ultimatum doesn't seem to be working," Clary observed as Sam joined him.

"Yeah, but this'll make a hell of a sidewalk sale." Sam cupped his hands around his mouth. "Hey, Lem, Clary and I haven't eaten yet. If you're going to be in there for a while, could you toss out a couple of steaks?"

A plastic-wrapped package of meat skidded out onto the boardwalk at Sam's feet.

"Humor isn't helping the situation either," Clary said, when the garbled noises behind him proved to be Owen Keller on the verge of apoplexy.

"Who's joking?" Sam asked. "Lunch was a long time ago."

"C'mon, Lem," Clary yelled. "Owen isn't to blame for your problems, so why are you taking it out on him?"

For the first time, silence reigned. No smashing sounds came from the store, nothing flew through the broken windows, and the crowd fell remarkably quiet.

Taking it as a positive sign, Clary stepped carefully out of hiding. Then, *splat!* An egg hit him full in the chest.

"I see he's made it to the dairy aisle," Sam observed as another egg whizzed by Clary's face.

"That's it." Clary refused to run, even though he had to brave a veritable storm of projectiles as he strode by the shattered windows on his way to the door. By the time he got there, his uniform looked like a fruit salad had exploded on him, and he'd taken another egg to the back of his neck. Besides stinging like hell where it hit him, most of the egg dripped down inside his collar before he could scrape it off.

"Deputy, wait!"

Hearing Ellie Reed's voice didn't help his temper any.

But at least it brought Lem to a cease fire. "Dr. Ellie?" he called out.

"Lem?" She picked her way through the debris until she stood next to Clary, one slim hand resting on the doorjamb of the market. "What are you doing?"

"I'm heeding your advice, ma'am," Lem said in a tone that sounded like a tug of the forelock went along with it.

Ellie glanced sideways at Clary, not quite meeting his eyes. "He must have misunderstood our conversation."

"Conversation?" Clary hung his head. "You're the one

who set him off? You're going to have to watch what you say to people from now on. I think you should probably avoid talking to people altogether, at least for a little while."

Ellie gave Clary a long, disgusted look. "The only way that's going to happen is if you trail me day and night, and run interference for me."

"Day and night? What do you think, Clary?"

"I think you're an idiot, Sam."

"I think I should talk to Lem," Ellie said.

"You may have meant well, but something you said put Lem in that store."

"Then something I say might get him out." She didn't wait for Clary's approval, stepping to the side so she stood in front of the broken window. "Lem?"

Clary squashed the urge to pull her back in case Lem got the notion to bean her with something. In his heart he knew she was safe. Lem Darby might be a shoplifting vandal, but he wouldn't hurt a woman.

"What are you doing in there?" she called out to Lem.

"I'm doing what you told me, Dr. Ellie. You said I should search inside myself, discover my special talent and find a way to make it happen."

Ellie glanced at Clary, her eyes widening as she took in the crowd behind him—and spotted Luke. She was momentarily sidetracked because she could've sworn her brother was standing with a teenage girl. And that teenage girl didn't seem as interested in what was going on at the market as she was in Luke.

"Dr. Reed?"

She focused her attention on the deputy sheriff and their predicament. "Keep them back," she whispered, "Lem is going to feel foolish enough once this is over without knowing the whole town heard every word he said."

"So?"

"So you wouldn't want another incident like this on your hands because someone teased him, would you?"

"I don't see how he's going to avoid being teased," Clary said, but he caught Sam's eye and jerked his head toward the crowd, the two of them joining ranks to nudge the townspeople to keep out of hearing distance. He left Sam to babysit and returned to Ellie's side with a signal from her to keep silent.

"I suggested you discover your inner talent and find a way to realize it, Lem. What does this have to do with that?"

"Well... I need money, and Owen's been overcharging me for years, so I thought I'd borrow a few dollars. I was going to pay him back after..."

When Ellie looked back at him, Clary lifted one shoulder in a you-got-me shrug. "After what?" she asked Lem.

"After I get to New York and sing in my first Broadway show. Maybe I'll get some respect around here when I'm rich and famous."

He said it so quietly they had to look at each other before they believed what they'd heard. A laugh burst out of Clary. About three seconds later, a coconut cream pie plastered him smack in the face.

Clary wiped the goo out of his eyes just in time to duck a new barrage of missiles, compliments of Sara Lee. "That's it." He took his shirt off and wiped his face with it, then wrapped it around his arm, choosing not to glance at the crowd when the noise level kicked up. It wouldn't help his frame of mind to see mature women hooting and hollering over the sight of him in his undershirt. "Talk to Lem," he told Ellie. "Keep him busy."

Clary ran his protected arm around the edge of the window frame. He was cutting his shirt to ribbons, but he got the glass cleared in a matter of seconds and was lifting his leg to step into the store when Ellie gripped his arm.

"What are you doing? I've almost convinced him to come out on his own."

"The hell with that." Clary brushed her hand off. "He's coming out of there now."

"Wait." She reached for his shirt, but her hands slipped and ended up curled around the waistband of his pants.

He went still immediately, one leg inside the window, the other out. His gaze streaked to hers, held, heated, before he looked down at her hands.

She let go, closing her fingers over palms that felt as if they'd been burned and shoving them behind her back. "This is partly my fault."

"Partly?"

"This is no time to assign blame. Give me a chance to get him out of there with at least some of his dignity intact."

"He's not the only one who's going to hear about this tomorrow," Clary pointed out.

Ellie tuned in to the jeers of the crowd and realized Lem wasn't the only one being ridiculed. Lem was already a semicomical figure in Erskine, but Clary had pie on his face, literally and figuratively, and his reputation would make him a much bigger target. The only way for him to redeem himself now was to bring Lem out himself.

But if either of them got hurt because of the advice she'd

given Lem… She couldn't bear the possibility of it. "I'm going in, too."

"Fine, Lem'll probably be calmer if you're there. He seems to trust you."

Ellie was so surprised to hear him agree with her that he was gone before she thought to scramble in after him. There was a great deal of crashing around, some swearing, but by the time she located the two men in the gloom inside the store, Clary already had Lem in handcuffs and was leading him to the door.

"I'm sorry," she murmured to Lem. "Where are you taking him, deputy?"

"He'll be in the basement over at the sheriff's office." At her appalled look, he added, "It's a jail, not a dungeon— and it's got more room than my apartment, so don't look at me like I'm subjecting him to cruel and unusual punishment. Besides, he ought to feel right at home there. It's full of canned goods for the food drive."

Ellie thought it politic not to respond. Clary deserved to be ticked off. "I'll come over and see you in the morning, Lem."

Clary unlocked the door and Ellie went out first, Lem close behind her. Clary stepped out last, right into a puddle of pureed banana.

He might have saved himself if he'd held on to Lem, but he didn't want to take him down, as well, so he pushed him into Ellie. She grabbed on to Lem's arm and dragged him to one side as Clary went down like a felled redwood, flat on his back. His breath whooshed out, and although he instinctively curled forward, his head came down hard on the raised threshold.

"You were right, Clary, somebody did get hurt," he heard Sam say as pain exploded through his skull.

The last thing he saw was Ellie bending over him. The last thing he heard was her voice, saying, "Try to stay awake, Clary."

His last thought, as blackness consumed him, was how much he liked hearing her say his name.

Chapter Six

The first thing Clary saw when he opened his eyes was water-stained acoustical ceiling tile. It took him a moment to figure out where he was; he'd been in Doctor Tyler's clinic dozens of times, only he'd never seen it from quite this angle before.

"He's awake."

Sam's voice. Clary turned his head—too fast, as it turned out, because the room spun and he had to close his eyes before his stomach rebelled.

"Concussion," Doc said succinctly. "The nausea confirms it."

As if Ellie had needed that confirmation. Under the tan, Clary's face was a sickly gray, his skin clammy, his eyes half-closed despite the fact that he was fighting to keep them open. "Lem?"

"Trust you to worry more about your job than your own noggin," Sam said to him. "Mike Shasta took Lem to jail."

"Can't leave him alone." Clary rolled onto his side, groaning slightly as he tried to swing his legs off the gurney.

"No you don't," she said, coming over to stop him. It

was only further proof of his injury that he let her. "Luke, why don't you and Sam go into the waiting room."

"Man," Luke said, "something interesting happens and I get sent off."

"I can understand why the kid has to leave, but why me?" Sam complained.

"Take it as an opportunity to get acquainted with your new intern," Doc said.

Sam looked at Luke, then at Ellie, a slow smile dawning on his face. "C'mon, kid," he said, giving Luke a friendly shove. "First lesson as my intern, I don't like to repeat myself." He looked over his shoulder at Ellie. "At least not where work is concerned."

Luke glanced back, but he didn't say anything before he walked out.

"'S the whole town here?" Clary mumbled.

"Sam and Luke just left," Doc replied calmly, "but Dr. Reed is still here, of course."

"Don' want her here."

"That's not what Sam said." Doc winked at Ellie. "Half the town wanted to pitch in to get you over here, but Sam said you'd only allow him and Ellie to help you."

Clary had a fuzzy memory of walking to the clinic with Sam propping him up on one side, Ellie on the other. "Sorry, too heavy…."

"No, you don't," he heard Ellie say. "You can't go to sleep."

He felt her hand on his cheek and smelled her perfume, faded after a long day so that most of what came through to him was woman, naturally sweet and completely intoxicating. He turned his head into her hand and kissed her palm, murmuring sleepily against her soft, warm skin. It felt so good to let his troubles and responsibilities go, to forget about Lem Darby and Owen Keller and rest in the knowledge that Ellie was there at his side.

Slapping him.

"Hey!" He reared up, only to have her push him back down.

"You have a concussion. You can't go to sleep."

"Sure I can. And if I'm lucky, I'll wake up in the morning and discover this whole fiasco has been a nightmare."

"You'll be lucky if you wake up at all. Ever."

He tried to sit again, so Ellie slammed both hands on his chest and leaned her weight on him. And found her face inches from his broad, hard-muscled chest covered only by a thin white undershirt. The scent of him rose to seduce her and the heat of him soaked into her palms, making her senses swim and her stomach flutter.

"Ellie," Clary said hoarsely. "Let me up."

She lifted her gaze to his and saw that she wasn't the only one feeling things she shouldn't be feeling. Tearing her eyes away from him she said, "If you get up too quickly you're liable to be dizzy, and if you go down, Doc and I won't be able to catch you."

"She's right about that." Doc laid a hand on Clary's shoulder to keep him flat on his back. "But I think it'll be okay if you sleep, son, as long as someone keeps an eye on you tonight. You can come to my house and use the spare room."

"You have clinic hours tomorrow," Ellie reminded her uncle, then kept talking right over his protest. "You can't possibly get enough sleep if you're waking up to check on Clary every hour or so, and if you're tired tomorrow you're putting your patients at risk. It'll have to be me."

"Makes sense," Clary chimed in.

Doc looked at Ellie, then Clary, both of whom made a point not to look at each other. "You're right, of course." He turned away, but Ellie had the sneaking suspicion it was to hide a smile rather than hurt feelings. "There's a bed in the back room—"

"I'm going home," Clary insisted.

Sam chose that instant to reappear. "I knew you'd say that," he told Clary. "That's why I went and got my pickup. I'm not hauling your big carcass around anymore on foot."

"Good thinking," Doc said. "Clary has a mild concussion—he won't be able to walk home. And since Ellie has offered to keep an eye on him tonight, you can make sure she doesn't have any trouble getting him up the stairs to his apartment."

That stopped Sam, but only for a second or two. "What about the kid?"

"I'm not a kid," Luke said hotly. "I can take care of myself."

"Sure," Sam said before the silence could become awkward. "But it makes more sense for you to come with me. Tomorrow's Saturday, which means it'll be a full day. If you bunk at my place tonight, Luke, we can get an early start in the morning."

Luke stuffed his hands in his pockets and shrugged.

"If you'd rather stay home tonight, Luke, you can take the car over to Sam's in the morning." Ellie reached out to her brother but he moved away.

Yet again she'd gotten caught up in her own drama and left her brother to fend for himself, and this time it was in a new community where he didn't really know a soul. Ellie looked up and found Clary watching her, the sympathy and understanding on his face too much for her to bear. She didn't want him feeling sorry for her. She didn't want anything from him, except to make sure he got through the night. Her conscience was already carrying around enough baggage.

CLARY WOKE UP to the shrilling of the alarm clock, not the quiet, comforting presence that had brought him to a light doze at intervals through the night, then soothed him back to sleep with gentle strokes and soft murmurs.

His loft apartment had only one large room besides the bathroom, but he didn't need to look around to know he was alone. The place felt as empty as it always did, nothing out of the ordinary. He was the one who felt different, disappointed.

He showered and dressed in record time, barely pausing to pop some extra-strength aspirin against the extra-strength ache behind his eyes before heading out the door. He stood there on the steps to the sheriff's office for a minute, feeling instantly lighter and happier. For the first time in years, he looked forward to something besides getting through another day. He looked forward to seeing Ellie.

The screech of brakes interrupted his musing, and it occurred to him that it was probably the sight of him standing there smiling like a fool that was wreaking havoc on traffic. "How about some pie, Clary?" someone called from one of the slow-moving cars.

Clary lifted a hand in acknowledgment and put his feet in motion. There was no way to outrun the full glory of Erskine's sense of humor, but he could wear it out. Which, from the sound of it, would take some doing.

He headed for the diner, out of duty if not hunger, and because he didn't think it was a good idea to see Ellie before Erskine got the riot at Keller's Market out of its collective system. He had a feeling she wouldn't be able to laugh off the jokes as easily as he could.

"Have a nice trip?" was the most frequent comment yelled out to him from the open doorways of the shops he passed and the open windows of the cars that passed him. "Hey, Clary, you got a new deputy?" and "Now that Dr. Ellie's in town, you can take a vacation," were pretty popular, too.

About the time he hit the corner of Main Street and the Interstate that ran across the edge of town, Maisie Cunningham shouted, "Hey, Clary!" in the same kind of voice she used to cut through the din of a wall-to-wall Saturday night crowd at the Ersk Inn. "The Ladies' CHAT group is still collecting food for the needy," Maisie said as she caught up to him. "Why don't you donate the uniform you were wearing last night? I bet it could feed a family of four for a week."

"Not your family, Maisie," he shot back, grinning.

The streets weren't teeming, by any means, even on a Saturday morning, but the people who were within earshot laughed, and most of them stopped what they were doing and gathered around. In Erskine, you took your entertainment where and when you found it.

"Too bad I wasn't at the market last night," Maisie said, not in the least insulted by Clary's comment. "Maybe I could've gotten Earl to toss some canned goods my way."

"With what Keller charges, it's a wonder somebody didn't loot the place before this," Mabel Erskine-Lippert observed.

There was a general rumble of agreement, stories flying back and forth about this incident of price-gouging or that instance of Owen tipping the scales in his favor.

"Seems to me Lem did us a favor," Mabel concluded.

Maisie jammed her hands on her hips. "How do you

figure? It's at least fifty miles to the nearest market. With gas prices what they are, and my car being what it isn't, meaning reliable, I can't make that trip every week."

Again, voices rose in agreement, the changeable nature of Erskine public opinion blowing, as it always did, hot and cold depending on the most recent argument.

"Then go every other week," Mabel said firmly. "Or carpool."

"Now folks—"

"Hush, Clary." Mabel turned her back to him with absolute confidence that he would obey her instantly.

And he did—not because she intimidated him, but because he'd seen it was too late to stop the momentum of the crowd.

"Even after Keller's reopens, we should keep carpooling for a while. Mark my words, it'll only be for a few weeks, a month at most. Owen Keller will drop his prices the minute he realizes we're serious. There's nothing that man likes less than losing money."

As he'd thought, Mabel had weighed the merits of the plan and decided on the best course for everyone involved—including Owen Keller. Owen wouldn't enjoy the boycott, but once he started charging fairer prices, he'd get less grief from the people in town. Which wasn't going to make him any more charitable toward Lem Darby.

Clary blew out a breath and left the townspeople to their insurrection. Lem was waiting for his breakfast, and considering he had bad news to deliver along with the food, the least Clary could do was not keep him waiting any longer.

He barely had time to take a seat at the counter in the diner before Edie brought over a piece of coconut cream pie and the place erupted in laughter. Clary dug in without batting an eye. Coconut cream wasn't his favorite, but it was better in him than on him.

Edie took out a pad and asked, "Is that the only thing you're having for breakfast, Clary?" She indicated the pie with her pencil. "Or do you want something else?"

Like the same meal he'd ordered every morning for as long as he could remember? "I need breakfast for Lem," he said, deciding to give his stomach a little while longer to get over the concussion. "Pancakes, two eggs over medium, wheat toast, ham."

"Sure thing. How about I get you some coffee while you're waiting?"

"That'd be good, thanks."

But Edie only stood there.

"Was there something else?"

"The new doctor." Edie set her pad down. "Is she really a psychiatrist?"

"She was in Los Angeles, but she says she's only going to practice regular medicine here."

"Oh. If I made an appointment with her at the clinic— I mean, I'm not sick or anything, but do you think she'd talk to me about something personal?"

If Lem Darby's current predicament was any indication, all Edie had to do was run into Ellie on any street corner and she'd be happy to hand out advice. No matter how reluctant she claimed to be, when it came right down to it, she simply couldn't seem to say no to anyone with a problem. Which could spell real trouble in a town like Erskine. And trouble was Clary's jurisdiction. Sam was right about that much.

"Clary?" Edie tapped on the counter to get his attention. "You want anything else?"

"Sorry, Edie. Yeah, I need to order Lem some lunch." He plucked a menu from the countertop holder, but she made opening it unnecessary.

"The grilled ham and cheese sandwich, and the tuna melt are his favorites," she said as she slipped the pencil from behind her ear and poised it over her order pad. "He usually takes a salad instead of fries, says it keeps him from getting sluggish in the afternoon."

Clary caught himself staring again. Two minutes ago she couldn't remember his usual breakfast, and he'd been ordering the same thing every morning for the better part of ten years. Yet here she was rattling off Lem Darby's preferences without a single eye roll. And why would she know what Lem liked for lunch when the man was usually off delivering the mail in the middle of the day?

"So? What's it gonna be?" she asked, her eyes meeting his without so much as a wobble.

"Why don't you decide? And if you could run it over to Lem when you have a chance, I'd appreciate it."

"Sure thing, Clary." The ten he took out of his wallet disappeared into her apron pocket. Not everything had changed.

It just felt that way.

Chapter Seven

Clary patrolled his town twice a day, seven days a week, winter and summer. It always centered him, waving back to the toot of a horn, making sure doors were locked and smelling the aromas of dinner wafting through open screen doors.

This evening, though, he had a splitting headache, a wandering mind and an urge to alter his route so he could walk by the clinic earlier than usual. It helped to remind himself that a member of his family was sitting in jail, courtesy—at least in part—of the woman he wanted to *casually* run into.

His path took him by Keller's Market, where some workers from Plains City Glass were replacing one of the large front windows. Clary opened the shop door, just in time to hold it for a tall, well-dressed man on his way out.

"My insurance adjustor," Owen explained. "There's a hefty deductible."

Which the dent-and-ding sale Owen had going would help with, if anyone wanted to buy a half-empty container of baby powder at what looked to be nearly full price. Maybe the town's boycott wasn't such a bad idea after all. Owen obviously hadn't learned anything the night before.

"I'm glad to hear you're insured. Lem is bound to get some jail time. At least ninety days. It'll be a while before he can pay whatever the judge orders in the way of damages."

"It's not about the money."

Now there were five words Clary had never expected to hear out of Owen Keller's mouth. "What's it about?"

"No offense, Clary, but Lem's been getting away with murder for as long as I can remember."

"Petty thievery, and you overcharged Lem to compensate. I should point out that there's probably something illegal about *that*."

"Maybe so, but if you charge me you'll have to charge the rest of the merchants in town, and I don't believe you're willing to do that. Besides, if Lem pays for what he did this time, he might think twice before he wrecks somebody else's place."

"He didn't mean to hurt anyone."

Both men turned and there was Ellie, standing in the doorway, the workmen staring at her through the newly installed glass.

"I'll be happy to pay whatever losses your insurance company doesn't cover," she said, stepping farther into the store.

"It wasn't your fault, Dr. Reed." Owen scuttled to the window and waved his pudgy arms to get the workmen moving again. "Lem's the one who trashed my store."

"He has a real problem, Mr. Keller."

"Owen."

"Owen. Kleptomania is an illness, and overcharging him all these years may have contributed to the feelings of helplessness that caused his illness."

He started to bluster out a defense. Ellie laid her hand on his arm and he sputtered into silence, going red in the face. "I realize you have a business to run, but don't you think there's some way we can work this out without keeping Lem in jail? Reparation? Community service?"

"That's not up to Owen," Clary said. "It's up to the judge."

"Big surprise to discover you feel that way, Deputy," Ellie said without looking at Clary. "If you don't press charges," she continued to Owen, "it won't have to go before a judge."

"But—"

Clary cut Owen off. "That would send the wrong message."

"You think a sudden crime wave is going to break out if you don't throw the book at Lem?"

"It's not just Lem. Your brother didn't get into trouble, either."

She faced Clary, hands on her hips, fire in her eyes. "Luke didn't do anything wrong."

"The kids in this town are hearing differently, and whether it's the truth or not, they're going to believe the sensationalized version of the story."

"And they don't know right from wrong? They're all going to turn into shoplifting vandals because of Luke and Lem?"

"Of course not."

"Then this is just about rules and laws and what you think should happen."

"No—"

"Yes, it is." She plucked Lem's arrest papers out of Clary's hand, took a second to peruse them and then brandished them in his face. "There's no such thing as middle ground with you. You probably have boxes on your desk labeled Right and Wrong, glued together so there's no room for maybe between them."

"I ought to have one labeled Good Intentions Gone Bad."

"At least I was trying to help Lem, which is more than I can say for you."

"I want to help Lem, too—"

"We're glad to hear you say that, aren't we, Owen?"

"Well…" Owen's gaze darted around the store, taking in the half-empty shelves, the food stains on the walls, the one still-empty window socket.

"Lem has his problems, but he's a good man, isn't he?" Ellie asked keeping her attention focused on Owen Keller.

She was staring at him with such patient certainty that he'd see it her way, Clary wasn't surprised when Owen nodded mutely.

"Then it's all settled," she said with a smile that had Owen blushing again.

"If Lem agrees to help with the deductible," he said, "I suppose I can meet him halfway."

"Without formal charges?" Ellie pressed.

Owen nodded. "But he has to do community service."

"Thank you, Owen," Ellie said, tearing the arrest papers in half and handing them back to Clary. "You won't be sorry."

Clary stood there, staring down the ruined remains of two hours of laborious typing. "I have a copy of the complaint in my office, Owen. You can still sign it."

"And have her come back in here for something besides groceries? No, thanks."

"Yeah, she's kind of stubborn when she gets her mind made up."

"You can say that again. If there's a next time, I'll just agree with her from the start. Save myself some time."

Clary nodded, stuffed the torn papers into his back pocket and headed out the door. He caught up with Ellie just as she was rounding the corner at the end of the block. She quickened her pace. Clearly she didn't want company. Clary wasn't in a hint-taking mood, so he lengthened his stride to match hers.

"How's your head?" she asked.

He snapped his mouth shut over what he'd been about to say. "Aching, but I took something for it," he said, remembering the reason he'd been so eager to see her earlier. "I wanted to thank you for last night."

"That's not necessary."

"You couldn't have gotten much sleep."

"It was my choice, Deputy."

"I'd think you could call me Clary after spending the night with me."

She gave him a sidelong glance. He caught the amusement in her eyes, mixed with a touch of uneasiness. She'd very neatly derailed him from continuing their...discussion about Lem, he saw now, but she didn't like the direction the conversation was going. Unfortunately, he'd always been too direct and literal a man to play that kind of game with a woman, and she was too good at reading people for him to be anything but direct. "Why did you leave?"

"You woke every time... Obviously you were okay, and I didn't think you'd want the whole town seeing me come out of your house in the morning."

"You don't think they're going to find out, anyway?"

"Yes, well, I do have other patients, Deputy."

If she was intending to zing him, being termed one of her patients did the job. "Including Lem?"

"I don't consider Lem a patient."

"And yet you felt a need to treat him."

"When Lem asked for my help, I couldn't ignore him."

"Like I did, you mean?"

"Meaning Lem has the kind of problem that only gets worse if it's not dealt with."

"So letting him get away with the shoplifting all this time didn't help."

"No, and while we're on the subject, why did you? You were ready to arrest Luke on the say-so of one woman, who in my opinion is nearsighted. But you know for a fact that Lem was shoplifting on a regular basis and yet you turned a blind eye."

"Because it's Lem. Everyone knows he doesn't mean any harm."

"And Luke is an outsider."

"He was a stranger," he corrected her. "He's also a kid, which is why I asked you to get involved. You assured me he didn't have a problem."

"I also assured you he didn't steal. But then I'm an outsider, too."

"That has nothing to do with it."

"All appearances to the contrary."

Clary snorted. "Are you sure you weren't a lawyer in Los Angeles?"

Ellie allowed herself a small smile. Otherwise, she didn't answer. As she'd known, Clary felt a need to fill the silence.

"We might have turned a blind eye to Lem, but he didn't have a meltdown until you psychoanalyzed him."

"Lem had a 'meltdown,' as you put it because he'd reached a breaking point long before I spoke with him. The signs were all there, if you knew what to look for."

"And I didn't." Whatever he'd been feeling before, he was downright angry now.

"I'm not saying you should have known, Deputy, but Lem was crying out for help."

"And you figured nobody else was listening. I thought you weren't going to practice psychiatry in Erskine."

"Not in the pure sense of it, but being a doctor, any kind of doctor, involves a bit of psychology, just like law enforcement involves compassion."

"Lem isn't the only one with a problem," Clary said through clenched teeth, "and you're not the only one sympathizing with him. Owen is about to find out that half the town is boycotting his store to get him to bring his prices down."

"And he'll blame Lem for that, when he should be blaming me?"

Clary didn't say anything, which was as good as agreeing with her. Ellie shook her head, hating the fact that she'd been thinking of him as *Clary*—as if there was a difference between Clary and Deputy Sheriff Beeber. Sure, he'd gone to Keller's Market to get Owen to sign the complaint papers, because Owen was the injured party, and there was no question that Lem was guilty. But in Clary's mind, so was she. "I wouldn't have spoken to Lem about his problems, but he seemed so lost and unhappy. He needed to make a change, but he was afraid."

"So you gave him a little pep talk, which landed him in jail."

"That's not what I expected would happen."

"The fact is, you don't know what will happen when you mess with someone's mind."

Ellie felt all the blood drain out of her face. "I don't mess with minds."

"And what if someone else comes to you with a problem—say Edie Macon, for instance? You think you can do something about the eye rolling?"

"A habit like that is—"

"None of your business."

"But it might help her to talk about why—"

"She does it because she thinks men are attracted to helpless women. If she believes men are that easily led, she must think we're all stupid."

"And maybe if I—"

"Stay out of it, Edie will eventually figure it out on her own."

"Are you ever going to let me finish a sentence?"

"Sure. As long as it begins with 'you're' and ends with—"

"—an idiot. Maybe Edie isn't so far off the mark in some cases."

He shot her a look. "I don't have any fancy college degree, but I have the sense—"

"Sense!" Ellie jerked to a halt in the middle of the walkway. "I didn't invite people to bring their problems to me."

Clary grimaced, tucking his thumbs into his police belt. "You're right. If I hadn't announced you're a psychiatrist, it wouldn't even be an issue."

Ellie let that stand for a second or two, but as tempting as it was to let him blame himself, it wasn't entirely fair. "You might have accelerated the problem, but in the end it wouldn't have mattered," she said. "I'm a doctor. People are going to bring me their problems, and there's no way to isolate the physical and psychological."

Clary didn't look very happy about her take on the situation.

She started walking again. "There's not a lot you can do about it, short of locking me up and throwing away the key."

"That's not a bad idea," he said. "How much trouble can you get into when there's little more than a cot in the room?"

Their eyes met and the air between them seemed to incinerate. Clary looked away and so did Ellie. *Not good,* she thought, *not good at all.* The last thing either of them needed was to get personally involved. Clary wouldn't want to be with a woman who had what she had weighing on her conscience. And she didn't want anyone. "You have an awfully low opinion of people in this town."

"No, I don't."

"Yes, you do. You talk about them as if they're children who can't be trusted to put one foot in front of the other without getting into trouble."

"You've been in town for a couple of weeks and you're an expert?"

"I've known you less time than that and I already know you see everything as a question of right and wrong. You're stubborn, inflexible, condescending, but most of all you're afraid—"

Clary opened his mouth to defend himself.

"Afraid," Ellie repeated right over top of him. "You're afraid to find out that maybe the people in Erskine can get along just fine without you now and then, and that you'll have to find something else to do in your spare time."

"She's got a point," Maisie Cunningham, who happened to be passing by, contributed.

Maisie took one look at Clary's face and kept walking.

When he turned his stare on her, Ellie could see why, but she refused to be intimidated. She clasped her hands behind her back, hating that he'd made her tremble. "I get your message loud and clear, Deputy. I'll try to confine myself to medical assistance. And there's at least one person in this town you don't have to worry about me talking to unless it's absolutely necessary."

SAM PUSHED THROUGH the clinic door, yelling out, "Where's my favorite doctor?"

Ellie pasted a smile on her face as she came out of Doc's cramped office. "I didn't expect to see the two of you until tomorrow."

"We came into town for supplies."

"And food," Luke added.

"You should've told me this guy was the human stomach," Sam joked. "I thought I'd be answering a million questions, but I didn't think they'd all center on food."

Ellie laughed softly, relaxing enough to tuck her hands in the pockets of her lab coat.

"Want to hit the diner with us?"

"No, I…" She put a hand over her stomach. "I've got a couple hours of work left here and then I just want to go home and sleep. Do you mind dropping Luke off after you eat?"

"He's coming home with me again, if that's okay with you," Sam said. "One day on the job and already I can't live without him."

Luke snorted. "You want me around so I can do all the dirty work and heavy lifting."

"What about your homework?" Ellie asked.

"Done," Luke said, shooting Sam a sidelong glance that told her he'd made that a condition of spending Sunday with him.

"I'll have him home for dinner Sunday, if you don't need him for anything before then, Ellie."

"No. No, that's all right. I'm working around the house tomorrow."

Sam ambled over to the counter and leaned his elbows on it, grinning suggestively. "Sounds cozy. I could come over and help."

That brought a real smile to Ellie's face. "Honestly, I'll be fine. To tell you the truth, I'm kind of looking forward to an Erskine-free day."

Sam straightened. "What's going on?"

"Nothing."

Sam didn't seem convinced. "You didn't see Clary today, by any chance?"

"It's kind of hard to miss him. That man's everywhere."

"This conversation is fascinating and everything," Luke interjected, "but I have some stuff to do."

"I'm right behind you," Sam said.

Luke waved a hand as he disappeared through the clinic door.

Sam stared after him for a minute.

"Everything okay?" Ellie asked. "Luke seemed happier than I've seen him in a long while, but if it's not working out—"

"It went great, for a first day. We had a couple of touchy moments— Luke is a bit tentative with the bigger animals, and he obviously has a lot on his mind, but when he asks a question, he actually listens to the answer. Soaks up everything I tell him like a sponge. It's kind of flattering, actually."

"He's had a tough few years, Sam. Our parents died, and then our grandmother. He's going to see you as a sort of parental figure."

"I don't know about parental," Sam said, grinning, "but Luke's big brother, now, I might be convinced to give that a try—if you ever want to make it a package deal."

Ellie couldn't help but smile back. "I'm not ready for romance. But I could use a friend."

Sam sighed and shook his head. "You're breaking my heart, Ellie."

"Something tells me you'll survive, Sam."

THE OUTER DOOR of the sheriff's office slammed open with the kind of urgency that always made Clary cringe. Usually it meant something outlandish had happened in Erskine. But that was before Ellie and her brother came to town, he amended as he stepped out of his office and saw Luke Reed, hands planted on the front counter, a belligerent expression on his face.

"Did you talk to my sister today?"

"We can have this discussion when you calm down."

"Is that how you operate? You tick people off and then refuse to talk to them?"

Clary was silent, jaw flexing.

Luke leaned forward. "Answer me."

"I don't respond to demands. When you're ready to have a conversation, we'll have one."

"I want to pound your face in."

Clary had turned to go, but that brought him back around. "You want to try?"

"You've got me by fifty pounds."

"And about a foot, which means you'd wind up getting spanked. Appropriate, since you're acting like a five-year-old."

"Does it make you feel important to throw your weight around? I might deserve it, but you can't tell me Ellie did anything wrong."

"We had a discussion about what happened with Lem Darby—"

"Which you think is Ellie's fault. Did you give her a chance to talk or was it her job to listen?"

"Trust me, she gave as good as she got," Clary said.

"Do us all a favor and stay away from my sister. She has enough on her mind…"

"What's on her mind?"

"Where do I start?" Luke said, a bit too quickly. "We're new in town—and you people aren't that welcoming to begin with. Then you announce in front of everybody that she's a psychiatrist, and when Lem Darby goes postal, you blame Ellie." He shook his head in disgust. "And everybody thinks I'm nuts."

"Nobody thinks you're nuts," Clary said. "Disrespectful, but that's another story."

"Yeah, well, I guess you get all the respect you need from the hicks living around here, because you're sure not trying to earn mine or my sister's."

Luke spun on his heel and blasted through the door with the force of a small tornado, snapping it back against the outside of the building. *Flamboyant tempers, those Reeds,* Clary mused, following the kid to the door.

Clary watched as Sam met Luke halfway across the town square and said something that made Luke's shoulders slump and Clary's hackles lift. It hadn't taken Sam long to infiltrate Ellie's life—or at least get a healthy start. He was already friends with her brother; it would only be a matter of time before he made a move on Ellie.

That was fine with him, Clary decided. She'd made it clear that she didn't want him in her life in anything more than a professional capacity. That left him where he should have been all along. With a job to do.

Clary was in the middle of a call to a friend from the marines who'd landed in law enforcement in Los Angeles, when Sam knocked on his office door. "R-E-E-D," he said into the receiver, gesturing Sam in with a wave of his hand. "Lucas and Elena. There's no police record on either one, I already checked that out." He looked up and caught Sam, watching him with narrowed eyes. "There's no hurry, Ken. Thanks."

"What the hell do you think you're doing?"

"Your turn to yell at me, Sam?"

"If I thought it would do any good, I'd hit you over the head again. Why are you checking up on her?"

"I'm checking up on *them*," Clary corrected. "Something Luke said got me to wondering."

"It's a mistake. Ellie Reed is not the kind of person to be in trouble, Clary, and neither is Luke—not real trouble, anyway.

"And I'm supposed to put everyone in town at risk on your word, Sam?"

"I thought you already knew she had a valid medical license."

"She's hiding something."

"Yeah, Clary, she's hiding something. The way she feels about you."

That caught him off guard.

"And don't think it doesn't make me sick," Sam rattled on, "her being attracted to you when I'm around."

"Did she tell you that?"

"She didn't have to."

"Great, now *you're* psychoanalyzing people?"

"What's to analyze? I've known you your whole life, Clary. After the thing with Lem, you decided you needed to have a little chat with Ellie, right? You told her to confine herself to bodies—sick ones—and leave the minds alone."

"Something like that," Clary said, refusing to give Sam the satisfaction of knowing just how close to the truth he'd come.

"It doesn't take a psychiatrist to know that she wouldn't be as upset if there wasn't something involved besides your jobs."

"She was angry, not upset."

"You know criminals," Sam pointed out. "Women are my area of expertise."

"I can't argue with that," Clary said. He suspected that Ellie was attracted to him, but more than that? "We've known each other less than two weeks, Sam."

"Yeah, and you've spent most of that giving her a hard time. Who said women were logical?"

"It's too soon."

"So you're telling me you haven't been thinking of her? And I'm not talking about what happened with Lem. I'm talking about you taking one look at Janey when you got back from the army and never looking at another woman the same way. Until now."

"I've known Janey all my life."

"True, but what about Laura?"

Love at first sight? Clary snorted. It wasn't his thing. Sure, he'd met and married Laura fast. But he'd been in the service and there hadn't been time to deliberate. Not to mention he'd been young and a lot more inclined to burn first and think later.

There was definitely chemistry between him and Ellie. Even if he wanted to deny it, he couldn't forget that first instance he'd heard her smoky, sexy voice outside the Five-And-Dime. And when he'd seen her... There weren't words to describe what she'd done to him. But chemistry wasn't enough any more. He wanted more to a relationship. He wanted conversation and debate, laughter and quiet times, breakfast at the start of the day, dinner at the end, and a lot of togetherness in between. And he wanted honesty.

Letting his hormones override his sense of responsibility would be the worst kind of dishonesty, to himself and to the people who counted on him to look out for them. "The call's already made, Sam."

"So make another call and cancel the first one."

"There's something going on with Ellie or Luke, and there's no harm in making sure it's not something that will spell trouble for Erskine."

"Fine. Go ahead and blow it, Clary. You won't be happy until you do." Sam went to the door but he turned back when he got there. "And when she finally figures out what an idiot you are, I'll be there to pick up the pieces."

"Another notch on your bedpost, Sam?"

"Yeah. The last one."

Chapter Eight

Spring fever hit Erskine with a vengeance the last few days of May, playing havoc with teenage hormones and school attendance, and as a result, making a drastic dent in Clary's desk time. The changeable weather also brought an outbreak of colds and flu, meaning Drs. Reed and Tyler were running themselves ragged. And since it was calving season, Sam Tucker's veterinary practice was busier than usual. According to the grapevine, however, that didn't keep Sam away from Ellie.

With Luke working as his assistant, Sam had the perfect excuse for dropping in at the clinic, or talking to Ellie on the street. Or having dinner with her—twice in the last two weeks that Clary had heard of. Not that it was any of his business. Ellie had made that perfectly clear.

True to her parting comment, she hadn't spoken a word to him since their last…conversation. And Clary didn't push the issue. She didn't want to talk to him? Fine. She had her work and so did he, and unless those duties intersected, he'd stay on his side of the line she'd drawn.

This time of year, and especially this day of the week, there was plenty to keep him busy. Sunday afternoon in

Erskine was a social event, particularly in the spring. Those who lived on the outlying ranches and farms had been shut in for months. The first few weekends of truly decent weather brought them into town in droves. This being Memorial Day weekend added another dimension to the social frenzy. People came for church and stayed on, families bringing picnic lunches or treating themselves to a meal at the diner or the Erskine Hotel.

The streets clogged with traffic, as did the boardwalks, and every now and then spring fever got the better of a citizen's common sense. Sometimes Clary called in help from the sheriff's office. Right about now, though, he wanted to be busy. He wanted to be walking his town, dealing with the petty problems of its people and…running into Janey.

She stopped abruptly when she caught sight of him, and then she laughed and said, "Hello, stranger."

Clary waited for the old familiar tongue-tying, mind-scrambling surge of need that had always hit him around Janey, but all he felt was a pleasant spike in his mood. Janey's laughter was one of the things that had first attracted him to her; he couldn't have resisted it even if he'd wanted to. When he came back to live in Erskine, so much of his world had been dark and lonely and full of regret. Janey had almost always been laughing, and after a while she'd made him laugh, too.

"It's good to see you," he said. "How's Jessie?"

"She misses you."

His relationship with Jessie, Janey's little girl, had been practically that of a father and daughter. Until her real father came back to town. When Janey had told Clary the truth she'd been dancing around for years, that she would never love him in the way he wanted, Clary had pulled out of her life entirely. He'd had to for his own sanity. "I thought it would be best to let the three of you settle in as a family."

"But that's not the only reason you've stayed away."

No, it wasn't the only reason. Clary had spent a lot of time trying to make Janey love him, and it still stung a bit to know that someone else had succeeded where he'd failed. It wasn't as if Janey had planned to hurt him, though.

"I'm sorry for staying away so long," he said.

"You don't need to apologize."

"Let me say this, Janey. I never could understand why… I think I'm finally beginning to see… What you and Noah have is really special. It just took me a while to figure that out."

"Oh, Clary," she sobbed, and gave him a big hug.

"What's this all about?"

"I'm pregnant," she said, laughing and crying at the same time.

"Hell, Janey," he loosened his hold on her immediately. In his mind incipient motherhood took her from full-grown woman to porcelain doll. "I'm happy for you."

She put him at arm's length, searching his face. "Are you?"

Clary took a moment to look inside himself before he answered. He'd felt a twinge in his heart when Janey's news had first sunk in, regret for what he'd never have in his own life. "Yeah, I am, Janey."

"Well, you're going to have to come to dinner," she said, muttering, "stupid hormones," as she wiped her eyes. "I knew you'd realize in your own time that what you felt for me was only friendship, but Noah will never believe it unless he hears it straight from the horse's mouth. I think I'll invite Ellie, too."

"Ellie?"

"Ellie. The new doctor in town? I met her yesterday. I like her. Not because she's the one who gave me the good news—well, not only because of that. She's nice, but I get the impression she's not a pushover, and she has a great sense of humor. Oh, don't think that innocent shrug and stoic lawman expression is going to put me off," she added. "Everyone in town knows Dr. Ellie spent the night at your place after you hit your head."

"It was her fault," Clary said, "partly."

"Interesting viewpoint. You might want to keep it to yourself."

"Yeah, she didn't take it very well."

"Oh, Clary," Janey said again, shaking her head fondly. "Tell me you didn't have a talk with her."

He'd done a lot more than that, and after the first rush of anger had worn off, he'd regretted making that call to Los Angeles. Not because he didn't think he had a right to know what Ellie was hiding, but because he'd gone about it the wrong way.

If it had been anyone else in town, he'd have asked outright what was going on. But the people in Erskine trusted him to look out for their best interests. He didn't know Ellie, and she didn't trust him—or respect him, according to Luke.

Going behind her back wasn't exactly going to help him gain her goodwill, and it wasn't setting well on his conscience. That didn't mean he'd been wrong in asking her to stop dishing out instant advice. "You know the people in this town, Janey."

"I do, but she doesn't."

"All the more reason for her not to get involved. Sigmund Freud would probably have trouble figuring out this bunch, and Ellie doesn't have anywhere near that kind of experience."

"If she's responsible for what's come over Edie, just about every woman in this county will be lining up to thank her."

Clary followed Janey's line of sight, and there was Edie walking down the street. At least it looked like Edie—same big blond hair, same skintight, cheek-skimming shorts, and there was no mistaking the sashay in her walk. But when she got close enough for Clary to see her face, he did a double take. The usual heavy mask of makeup had been replaced with subtler shades of eye shadow and blush. Her lipstick was a warm, flattering pink and her blouse was buttoned to a respectable level, actually leaving something to the imagination. She waved and smiled, her eyes never once rolling back.

"How can you say that's a bad thing?" Janey said.

"Just give it time."

"You didn't used to be such a pessimist."

"I used to have some control over what happened around here."

"You don't really believe that."

"It felt like I had control."

Janey chuckled and stretched up on her toes to kiss his cheek.

"Does Noah have any idea this is going on?"

Clary turned around and saw Sara Devlin, third-grade teacher and Janey's best friend, coming up the boardwalk.

"Sara, there you are," Janey said.

"There I am! You were supposed to meet me at the diner a half hour ago."

"I'm not going to apologize."

Sara looked from one face to the other and smiled teasingly. "If you come and have lunch with us, Clary, you and Janey can continue your conversation."

And she could eavesdrop. "Thanks for the invitation, but there's something else I have to take care of." First he was going home, though. No way was he running this errand in his uniform. "Tell Jessie we'll go fishing sometime soon," he said to Janey.

"I'll do that," she called after him.

Noah knew she and Sara were watching him walk away, wondering what was going on with him and probably drawing conclusions he didn't want drawn. And Janey knew him way too well not to figure out what was happening—if she hadn't already. Why else would she tell him to bring Ellie to dinner?

He resisted the urge to set her straight; he knew Janey wouldn't spread her assumptions around town. And even if she did, there wouldn't be any truth to the rumors.

ELLIE HAD HAD days off in L.A., but never like this. Then she'd volunteered at the state mental hospital, or worked on a paper to be published in one of the medical journals, or if she'd stayed home, she'd have cleaned maniacally. Today she just wanted to be outside, and what a glorious day for it.

It was still breezy, so that even at noon she'd wrapped one of her grandmother's afghans around her shoulders before stepping out onto the wide back porch. The view of the valley behind her house was soothing. The orchard was half green, half white, just beginning to bloom. Green was slowly taking over the grassland, with a patch of wild-flowers here and there lending a splash of color. More flowers grew around the house—daffodils and crocuses in once-tidy beds that were now wonderfully untamed.

Ellie took a deep breath and closed her eyes, feeling something inside her, equally untamed, stretching and pushing to get out. Her life had been structure and respon-sibility and duty for so long, to Luke, her grandmother and her patients. She'd even felt an absurd need to prove some-thing to her parents. They'd been so proud of her when she was accepted into medical school. After their deaths she'd worked that much harder, determined to be the best, the youngest to reach the top of her field, the expert people consulted the world over.

And while she was focusing on her own greatness, she'd forgotten why she'd gone into psychiatry in the first place. To help people. She'd failed miserably.

At least in one respect, the Los Angeles medical com-munity was just like Erskine. Talk got around fast, scandal even faster. To her everlasting shame, she'd hightailed it out of town before anyone could come right out and call her what she'd already labeled herself. A—

"It looks like a painting, doesn't it?"

Ellie gasped, her hand flying to her mouth as if she'd been about to utter the rest of her thought with Clary standing there at the side of her back porch. "What do you want?"

"You're not going to yell at me again, are you? Because you did a pretty good job of it the last time I saw you, and then Luke picked up where you left off."

"Luke? I didn't say anything to him."

"He's your brother. You shouldn't have to say anything to him."

No, Ellie thought, apparently not. She'd worked so hard to keep her upheaval from showing, but she hadn't fooled Luke. And he'd raced to her defense. It made her want to smile. She managed not to. "If you came out here for an apology, Luke's not here. And even if he was, I wouldn't ask him to apologize."

"Is that what you think of me? That I'd expect him to apologize for defending his own sister?"

Ellie turned away, searching for peace in the one place she'd found it. But it wasn't there now, not with Clary standing five feet from her.

"I should be the one apologizing to you, anyway."

That caught her by surprise. "For what?"

He started to say something, then shook his head. "I know what Lem did wasn't your fault. I shouldn't have blamed you for it, and it was unreasonable to expect you to ignore someone who came to you with a problem."

"It was a knee-jerk reaction. You were upset about the situation, and you lashed out. It's completely understandable."

"And fitting, seeing as how I can't seem to be anything but a jerk when I'm around you."

She knew it was a mistake, but she looked at him, and made a bigger mistake by echoing the chagrined half smile on his face. He started around the corner of the porch, and for every step he took she took a step back—another knee-jerk reaction, this time to the way her heart pounded.

It was the jeans, she told herself, worn white at the stress points, as molded to him as the long-sleeved Henley, so that every muscle was clearly discernible. And he was all muscle. She tried to rattle off the names in her head, anything to ignore the same wild something that was still trying to push its way through the self-control she wore like body armor.

She came up short at the far end of the porch. Clary stopped, as well, on the other side of the railing, and she saw the same wildness in his eyes. She didn't dare think about the fact that he'd appealed to her from the second they'd met, how even butting heads with him had seemed to be just one of the steps in the strange dance they were doing. And she couldn't, whatever else she did, think about that look they'd shared the day they'd argued, with the idea of the narrow jail cot looming between them.

If she made the wrong move, she knew they'd both be lost. Luckily, she couldn't seem to make any move. She was frozen, her eyes locked with his for what felt like an eternity. And then one side of his mouth quirked up, not quite a smile, as his gaze panned the back of the house.

"I see they've started the work already."

Ellie pulled the afghan tighter around her shoulders, clutching it in the middle with both hands. She nodded, her heart so high up in her throat she couldn't have uttered a word to save her life.

"What are you having done?" Clary asked, as if that moment had never passed between them.

His control made it easier to find hers. "I'm pretty much leaving it to Ted."

Clary nodded. There were any number of carpenters in the area, but Ted Delancey was the best. "I couldn't tell anything had changed from the front," he said, studying the house Ellie had rescued from the twin terrors of dry rot and insect infestation.

A wide, rambling covered porch wrapped around the

front, sides and back. Chimneys jutted at either end, and dormer windows broke the austere line of the roof, giving the house a nice, balanced appearance that had always appealed to Clary's sense of tidiness.

He backed off a little, keeping his attention carefully focused on the changes so he wouldn't notice the way the midday sun turned Ellie's skin to gold, or that she wore denim like a second skin and yet the crocheted afghan she'd wrapped around her shoulders made her seem old-fashioned.

His heart kicked hard in his chest, his pulse raging with a steady, hollow roar in his ears. It took an absurd amount of strength to keep his hands at his sides when all he wanted was to reach for her.

It was why he'd fought not to think about the comforting gentleness of her touch and her voice in the night, or the time her eyes had met his when he'd mentioned that cot in the jail cell. He was decisive when circumstances called for it, when someone or something in his town was in danger. In all other areas of his life he preferred to be deliberate, to ponder and debate before he chose which way to step.

There was no pondering when it came to Ellie, no possible hope for a slow and calm examination of what she did to him. Just seeing her put him on the edge of something hot and dangerous. Something he was afraid to unleash.

He should've walked away, left her without a word and if she was insulted or hurt, all the better for them both. He didn't quite have the willpower for that. Even knowing it would bring him relief, he didn't want to leave her.

So, sweating, muscles tight and mouth dry, he concentrated almost desperately on the back of the house. The porch roof had been extended and strengthened to carry a walkout deck, and the second-story wall was lined with windows. "It looks great."

"Ted had a crew come in and put up the outer structure because he was afraid the weather would turn."

Her voice held enough of a chill to warn him to keep his distance, and tell him he'd made the right decision. His conscience had brought him to her door, but stronger urges kept him silent. She'd just started to warm up again. If he told her about the call to Los Angeles, he'd destroy any chance he had of friendship, let alone anything more. And he wanted more.

"Montana in May can be pretty unpredictable. Knee-deep snow one day and picnic weather the next," he said.

She nodded. "It's still pretty rough inside. There's a plumber and an electrician coming, but Ted is doing the finish work himself— Oh, I think I hear the phone."

She hadn't; they both knew it, and Clary knew it would be wise to get in his truck and hightail it back to town. Obviously he'd pushed her as far as she was willing to go. Still, he chose to follow her into the house.

The scent of freshly cut wood mixed with the sharper odors of paint and polyurethane. Bare stud walls were all that separated the kitchen from the dining room.

"Just my imagination," she said, looking anywhere but at him. "I guess I'm a little jumpy. On call, you know, expecting the phone to ring any second."

"Uh-huh."

"Maybe… I was about to make myself a late lunch. Unless you need to get back to town," she said, trying not to make it sound hopeful.

"It's not like I get the treat of a home-cooked meal every day," he said. "I'd be a fool to pass it up."

"Nobody's ever described my cooking as a treat. But I can open a can of soup and make grilled cheese."

Clary leaned against the counter in the kitchen. The sink took up most of the counter space along the still-intact outer wall and a two-burner hotplate occupied the rest.

"The stove wasn't much more than a nest for mice, so I had Ted take it out," Ellie said. "The refrigerator had to go, as well, but Luke and I are making do with this one." She bent to open a knee-high office fridge, taking out cheese, butter and bread. "I almost didn't bring it with me, but I'm glad I did." She knew she was rambling, knew it was a classic response to the disconcerting way he was watching her, but she let herself go.

Talking forced her mind onto subjects that were safer than the fact that his tall, strong body seemed too close, even when he was across the room. That he was wearing those damned jeans.

When he was in uniform it was easy to remember the reasons she had to keep her distance, but those jeans made him seem more approachable. Those jeans were probably the reason she'd invited him to lunch, she realized too late, wondering if he'd worn them to take her off her guard. And why.

On second thought, she didn't want to know the answers to those questions. She could think of only two reasons why he'd want her off balance, and both of them spelled trouble.

"Why don't you sit down?" she said quietly. "I think the two of us can survive an hour in each other's presence without arguing."

"Is there anything I can do to help?"

"There's not really enough room for both of us to be moving around." She went to the cupboard and took out two cans of soup, holding them up for him so he could see the names on the distinctive red and white labels. He pointed to one and she smiled slightly. Tomato was her favorite, as well.

"So tell me about yourself," she said, as she prepared the soup and began putting together the sandwiches.

"Not much to tell," he said with a shrug. "I grew up in Erskine, but there isn't a lot of opportunity around here for someone who doesn't want to be a rancher or farmer."

She sent him an amused look, which he returned. He definitely wasn't farmer material.

"When I turned eighteen, my dad wanted me to go to college, but college didn't seem to be the thing for me, either. I wanted to see the world, so I joined the marines."

His deep voice filled the room, and the strongest sense of...*rightness* washed over Ellie, a feeling of contentment she hadn't known since she was a little girl and happiness meant playing in the sun all day, then coming home to her parents' loving arms.

She listened to Clary talk, heard and comprehended his words, and lost them again as a need rose up in her, so powerful it was all she could do to keep moving so he wouldn't know how radically her life had just shifted. Here, in this torn-up kitchen, she got a flash of what it would mean to share her life with someone, to have dinner every evening and exchange stories of the day. It didn't matter what the surroundings were, if you dined on caviar and champagne or grilled cheese and tomato soup—as long as you were with someone you...loved.

Ellie looked over at Clary and thought about what it would be like to know the peace and solid security of a man who not only understood his place, but genuinely liked it and was content. She couldn't think of anything more wonderful. Was that why, suddenly, she wondered if she was falling in love with him? Was she feeling so warm toward him because this homey situation reminded her of things that had been missing from her life for a long time?

She'd have those things again, she told herself. She'd have a family and a place to belong, but it wouldn't be with Clary. He was the last man who would ever accept her for who she was, faults and all.

It really was too bad, she thought with a touch of sadness as she tuned back in to the conversation, because he'd undoubtedly be as dedicated, unwavering and loving toward a wife as he was toward his town.

"A couple of years into my first tour of duty I got married and, well, you know how that turned out."

"I can see that you're blaming yourself for her death."

"It was cancer. Nothing I could do about it. Except be there for her."

Before she could find something to say, anything that didn't sound like a platitude, the opportunity passed her by.

"My father ran the bank in Erskine," he said, "so after…all I wanted was to come home."

Because he'd needed the comfort of people who cared for him, of familiar places and circumstances that didn't offer any surprises. She kept the insight to herself, knowing he wouldn't welcome it. "You don't have any brothers or sisters?" she asked, sliding the sandwiches onto plates and bringing them to the table, which, belatedly, she realized she hadn't set.

"No, I was an only child. My parents retired to Florida while I was still in the marines. Sam wrote me that Erskine was looking for a deputy sheriff, and my tour was almost over by then, so I applied for the job." He laughed. "There weren't a lot of applicants. Me and Jess Hadley, and he's drunk half the time."

Ellie delivered two mugs of soup to the table, retrieved some spoons and napkins and took her seat. "If they'd had a thousand applicants, they couldn't have found anyone better," she said, smiling at the surprise on his face. "It's obvious you love the town and your job."

"It's home."

He loaded up his plate, oblivious to what he'd done to her. The bare simplicity of that word, *home,* the way he said it as if it answered every question in life, made her almost sick with loneliness.

"This must be a pretty big change from L.A.," he said.

"Yes, I lived in the big city my whole life."

"Were you happy there?"

"Most of the time." She missed the quiet nights spent with friends, sipping wine, laughing and talking at the end of the day or week. But those times had disappeared long before she moved; the people she'd thought were friends had stopped socializing with her, some of them because they'd passed judgment on her, others because they didn't know how to talk to her anymore. She'd as good as turned into a hermit. And then she'd left.

"It usually takes a lot to make someone leave everything familiar behind."

She picked up her soup mug and took a cautious sip, careful not to meet his eyes. "When our grandmother died, and Uncle Don called…in the city you are your job." *And*

when your job was taken away from you, you were no one.
"It wasn't enough."

"I've got news for you, you are your job here, too."

"And you're the living incarnation of law and order?"

He lifted a shoulder, let it drop.

"What happened with your wife… She wouldn't want you to spend the rest of your life punishing yourself, Clary."

"You sound as if you know what you're talking about."

"Just my compulsion to psychoanalyze," she said, hating the way he closed down. But it was better for them both. Getting into a relationship with Clary wouldn't only be wrong for her, it would be damaging to him. He'd lost his wife, and he'd lost Janey, if the gossip in town could be believed. The worst thing that could happen to him was having another affair go bad, and where she was concerned, there wasn't any other possible outcome. "Everyone in town is your friend, Clary. It's a part of what makes this place so charming."

"Charming." Clary shook his head. "That's not the way I'd describe Erskine—"

This time there was no mistaking the sound of a phone ringing. Clary reached for the cell phone at his hip. He didn't say more than "hello" and a couple of "uh-huhs," but his eyes met hers and her heart began to pound.

He flipped the phone shut and caught her by the arm. "You have to come with me."

Chapter Nine

"Wait a minute." Ellie struggled to get loose, but Clary hauled her through the house and out to the truck.

He opened the passenger door and said, "Get in."

"What's going on? Who's hurt?"

"Teenage girls," Clary said, exasperation in his voice.

"Teenage girls are hurt?"

"No, there's some sort of…ruckus at the Five-And-Dime." He skirted the hood and got in the SUV, barely waiting for her to climb in before he jammed it into reverse and backed out of her driveway in a shower of gravel.

"I haven't given anyone advice," Ellie said.

He glanced over at her. "I know."

"I hardly spoke to anyone all week, except for patients, and I promise you none of them were teenage girls."

"I didn't meant to imply that I thought this was your fault. There was a lot of background noise on the phone call, but near as I can tell it has something to do with teenage boys."

"What do you want me to do about it?" She braced herself as he screeched around the first corner into town.

"Talk to them."

"You talk to them. I'm a stranger. You've known them all your life."

"Exactly, and if past history is any indication they won't want to discuss their romantic troubles with me, even—"

He broke off but Ellie had no problem finishing the thought. "Typical man," she muttered. "Anything to do with feelings and you run in the other direction."

"It's not that—well, not entirely," he allowed. "You seem to have a way with people, if what you did for Edie Macon is any indication."

Ellie frowned, mostly to hide the pleasure it gave her to hear a compliment, no matter how vague, from Clary. Edie had come to see her at the clinic a few days ago, and they'd begun talking through her self-esteem issues. Since then, there was a definite improvement in her appearance and comportment, and if she'd had a hand in it, she was proud of herself. That didn't mean she wanted anything to do with this latest brouhaha. "Where are the girls' parents?"

"I don't know," Clary said as he threaded his way through traffic. "If they're in town, the kids avoid them like the plague, and the farm kids who have their license drive themselves and their friends in. Everybody keeps an eye on them."

"Not everyone," Ellie muttered. "You."

"It's my job."

"It's your job to be responsible for every teenage kid within a fifty-mile radius?"

"If one of them gets in trouble, I'm not about to wait for their parents to get here before I step in."

"Commendable, but you're asking *me* to step in."

"You're a doctor. This is an emergency."

"It's not a medical emergency." Thank heavens. "You told me not to get involved with anything but medical situations."

"I apologized for that, remember?"

"That doesn't mean you've changed your mind."

"Yeah. Okay. I changed my mind." He pulled up in front of the Five-And-Dime, parking the Blazer in the street because there weren't any spaces available. He shut it off and looked at her. "Feel free to talk to anyone you want about anything at all."

"Are you saying that because you don't want to deal with the cute little teenage girls?"

Clary opened his door. The cute little teenage girls were screaming loud enough to violate FCC regulations.

"Are you sure it's just an argument?" Ellie asked.

"Whatever it is, it's drawn a crowd."

The Five-And-Dime was bursting at the seams. People spilled out the doorway and others were plastered to the front window. Clary reached under the front seat and came up with a portable loudspeaker. He pressed the button and an ear-splitting shriek emerged from the deceptively small canister. Instantly, attention shifted from what was happening inside to what was happening outside, and when they saw it was Clary, a path magically opened to the front door.

"Oh, well, you've got things under control," Ellie said. "Maybe it would be best if I stayed here."

Clary didn't waste time arguing. He simply curled his hand around hers and towed her across the bench seat and out through the driver's side. "There's no way I'm going in there alone."

Ellie didn't know whether to laugh or scream. On the one hand, it was so endearingly ludicrous for a big, strong man like Clary to be leery of a couple of teenage girls. She, however, had good reason to be cautious. If she so much as opened her mouth and anything happened down the road, it would turn out to be her fault. She just knew it.

Of course, he gave her no choice, dragging her along in his wake like a piece of toilet paper stuck to the bottom of his shoe. That was the way people were looking at her, trailing behind Clary like some odd bit of flotsam he'd be surprised and embarrassed to discover he'd picked up. His views on psychiatry were pretty well known.

"Why don't you folks go on about your business," Clary said once they were standing in front of the store.

"I don't know, Clary, you're not wearing your uniform," a man in the crowd observed.

Gazes shifted from the action inside the Five-And-Dime to where Clary stood, so they could all marvel at the fact that he wore blue jeans instead of khaki cop pants. Unfortunately, that meant they were also now staring at Ellie behind him, and it wasn't long before some of those stares turned speculative. Erskine knew how to start a rumor, and it didn't take much.

"Maybe I should go talk to the girls," Ellie said, that ordeal seeming a lot more attractive, suddenly, than being identified as the reason Clary was out of uniform. "That's why I'm here, after all."

Causing disappointment could be a good thing, she discovered, although the townspeople pounced on Clary again now that she'd taken the entertainment potential out of her presence.

"You're not even wearing your badge," another unknown voice pointed out.

"Can you write tickets and arrest people without your uniform and badge, Clary?"

"I get called in the middle of the night often enough," he said, "and I'm not wearing my uniform and badge then."

There were hoots and hollers, a couple of women fanned themselves and one called out, "What *are* you wearing?" When Clary didn't answer, they began to speculate.

"I don't sleep naked," he finally said, another mistake that raised the boxers or briefs debate. He turned away, trying not to imagine that every female eye in the crowd was looking at his backside and wondering. And then the conversation switched to his handcuffs, and he decided his choice of underwear wasn't the worst thing they could be talking about.

Ellie, he saw, was taking it all in, arms crossed, grinning full out.

He drew her through the throng inside the store to the same old-fashioned soda fountain where Luke had been sitting the day he'd been sent home from school.

He gave the horn a toot and the three bickering girls went suddenly, blessedly silent. "Peggy," he said, indicating the girl standing behind the counter, wearing a white uniform and frilly pink apron. "Sue Ann." He tipped his head toward the girl standing to his right. "Cara." The girl to his left met his gaze head-on. "Girls, why don't you tell Dr. Reed what's wrong?"

That earned him three different expressions—sulky, sullen and defiant—and absolute silence. He nudged Ellie forward, directly into the line of fire.

"See, nothing wrong here," Ellie said. "Let's go." She tried to step back and found herself up against Clary. She should've moved, would have, but he spoke then. His voice was a quiet rumble in her ears, his body a warm, comforting presence behind her. By the time she realized she should be listening to his words rather than just enjoying the way they felt, it was too late.

The girls were shooting each other poisonous looks, and Clary prodded her again.

She looked over her shoulder at him.

"Say something," he mouthed at her.

"They're not going to open up with all these people here."

"It didn't bother them before we got here. I don't know what's going on," he said to the girls, "but I brought Dr. Reed to, uh, help you sort it out."

"There isn't a problem," Sue Ann muttered.

"Everything's okay," Peggy echoed.

"Sue Ann thinks Peggy is trying to steal her boyfriend," Cara said with a smirk.

Great, not only was she up against teenage angst, one of the girls was an agitator, to boot.

"As if I want to date a loser like Kyle, " Peggy said from her position behind the counter.

Cara jumped to her feet. "That loser is my brother."

"Well, that's what you call him."

"It's okay when I call him that, but not when you do it," Cara retorted.

Ellie, seeing no other choice but to get this over with as quickly as possible, stepped up to the counter between Cara and Sue Ann. "Why do you think Peggy is trying to steal your boyfriend?" she asked the latter.

"He comes in here every day after school for a vanilla shake—"

Peggy snorted. "So do half the kids in town, you moron."

"Okay, there'll be no more name calling." Ellie happened to glance over at Sue Ann just as she stuck her tongue out. "That doesn't solve anything, either."

The two girls continued to scowl at each other, but they both nodded. Cara looked as if she was having the time of her life.

Ellie took a deep breath, searching for a way to get to the bottom of the dilemma without causing any more trouble. "What did Peggy do that makes you think she's trying to steal your boyfriend?" she asked Sue Ann.

"It wasn't her, exactly," Sue Ann said sullenly. "Kyle talked to her in history. Twice."

"He wanted to borrow a piece of paper and I didn't hear him the first time," Peggy said.

"And he sat with her on the bus," Cara reminded everyone.

"The bus driver made him," Peggy protested. "The boys were sitting in the back of the bus…" She glimpsed at Clary and decided not to finish that comment.

"He winked at you, too."

"Shut up!" the other two girls shouted at Cara, at which point they launched into another free-for-all shriekfest.

"Seems to me he would do more than borrow paper and wink if he was interested in Sue Ann," Clary said to Ellie.

"I know grown men who consider a smile an undying declaration of love."

"Were any of them smiling at you?"

Ellie rolled her eyes, easing him aside with the back of her hand. "Look, girls," she said, "I don't know what's on this boy's mind, and obviously neither do you. The only way to sort this out is for you to have a long talk with Kyle, Sue Ann. Tell him how you feel about him and make sure he's as committed to your relationship as you are, and everything will be okay. If he doesn't feel the same way you do, then you're better off without him. And in the meanwhile, I'm sure Peggy has no intention of doing anything that would hurt you."

By the time she finished, all three girls were staring at her as if she'd sprouted antennae. For that matter so was everyone else in the place. And along with the confusion, she saw disappointment. Well, she asked herself, what had they expected? She was a psychiatrist for pete's sake, not a referee. And at least she was willing to roll up her sleeves and help solve the argument instead of turning it into a spectator sport.

Peggy and Sue Ann weren't hugging or anything, but they weren't exchanging death stares anymore, either. It seemed as if everything was going to be all right. Or it would've been, if not for Cara.

She elbowed Sue Ann. "You should apologize to Peggy. Not to mention my brother."

"It's okay," Peggy said. "No harm done."

"No harm? When Kyle hears about this, he's going to freak."

"Ohmigod." Sue Ann covered her mouth, her eyes filling with tears. "I have to explain this before he finds out about it from somebody else."

"You're not driving until you calm down."

Clary stepped in front of her, but she squirmed by him and darted through the crowd. He set off after her, but Sue Ann, being much smaller, was able to weave her way through the packed aisles a lot faster than he could manage. He got to the boardwalk, racing out into the street so he could see around his Blazer. What he saw was the wide chrome grill of Sue Ann's mother's big old Lincoln Continental.

Right before she sideswiped him.

Clary spun a full circle and wound up sprawled on the ground in a choking cloud of dust and blue smoke, ringed by a circle of heads backlit with the blinding brilliance of the sky. He couldn't make out faces, except for Ellie's. She was crouched beside him. Her soft hands ran up his arms and over his chest, around the back of his neck, gently kneading through his hair before she shifted to reach his legs.

"Someone's gone for Doc Tyler," she said when she noticed him watching her. "Tell me if it hurts anywhere."

It wasn't just the agony exploding in his side that made him hiss in his breath. "You come any higher and pain won't be the issue—at least not the kind you mean."

Chapter Ten

"This is getting to be a habit," Dr. Tyler said as he joined Ellie in the clinic's waiting room.

"A bad habit." She stifled a shudder when she thought about the way Clary had been sprawled out in the road a little while earlier. He could've sustained any one of a dozen fatal injuries being hit by a car, and a dozen more that would've been fatal in a town with no emergency medical facilities. And she'd been helpless.

"Clary's going to be fine, Ellie." Doc's hand closed, warm and comforting, over hers.

She squeezed his hand, then withdrew hers. Sympathy was hell on self-control. "I'm just glad you were home," she said. And that there had been no shortage of willing hands to get Clary to the clinic. She took a shaky breath, refusing to examine why Clary's state of being had gone from something she felt obligated to preserve to something that could consume her with blind terror. "I'm sorry we had to interrupt your quiet Sunday. Are you keeping Clary here tonight or should we get him to a hospital?"

"Neither. It was only a graze, Ellie. He'll be bruised, right down to the bone, but nothing's broken, or even sprained, for that matter. I would've thought you knew that before you chose to move him over here."

"I—I checked him over. Everything seemed to be okay, but…"

Doc sighed. "I'm beginning to wonder if I did either of us a favor by bringing you here."

Ellie sank into a chair. Doc took the one next to her, and this time when his hand closed over hers it wasn't in comfort. His grip was hard enough to bring her gaze to his face.

"After what happened in Los Angeles, I thought you'd be happier in a community that isn't so fast-paced and competitive. You have family here. You're young and resilient, and I believed it wouldn't be long before you got your feet under you again." He released her fingers, sitting back in his chair. "But you're getting worse, not better, Ellie. You've been calling me for more and more trivial diagnoses."

"That's rather harsh—"

"Two days ago you tried to get me to order a lung X-ray for a patient with a history of allergies."

"She's eight years old, Uncle Don. I only wanted to make sure we weren't overlooking anything."

"It's the height of pollen season. No matter what we prescribe, it's normal for the child to do some coughing and sneezing. Ordering a chest X-ray would needlessly alarm her parents."

"Has… Did someone call you?"

"No. None of the patients have noticed your lack of confidence yet. You're still new in town. They're probably comforted having your opinion confirmed by me."

"I'm comforted," Ellie murmured.

"You're afraid, and you're using me as a crutch. We're doctors, Ellie, not gods."

"If I thought of myself that way I wouldn't be so worried about making another mistake."

"Well," he sounded tired suddenly, "at least you can't punish yourself any more than you already are. And don't tell me you don't know what I'm talking about. It's obvious to anyone with eyes that you're interested in Clary."

Ellie began to speak, but he shushed her.

"Do you think denying yourself happiness will bring that boy back?"

"I'm not denying myself anything." Ellie got to her feet. "If I felt something for the deputy sheriff, and if he felt something for me, where would it go? Do you think Clary would be able to overlook what happened to one of my patients because of me?"

"I think you should give him the chance to decide what he can and can't live with. But you're not going to, are you?"

"I can't." Ellie wrapped her arms around herself. "When he finds out—"

"Why don't you just tell him and get it over with?"

Her mouth opened, but nothing came out except a little trickle of air. It was going to be bad enough when he discovered she was responsible for the death of a patient. She didn't want to be around to witness the moment.

"I don't know why I thought you could trust Clary when you can't even trust yourself yet."

"I need time, Uncle Don. I promise it'll get better if you give me some time. It's only been a few weeks—"

"It's been almost a year since it happened, Ellie. It's not going to get any easier until you make up your mind that you deserve to have a life again, and that your life is going to include risk. Don't let fear dictate your actions for so long it gets to be a habit."

She nodded, but she was wondering if it was already a habit. "Thank you, Uncle Don, for everything."

"Just keep in mind that I was looking forward to learning how to play golf."

Ellie gave him a wobbly smile. "I shouldn't let fear dictate my actions, but guilt is okay?"

"Right, what am I thinking, laying more guilt on you?" Doc pulled her to her feet and enveloped her in a hug.

Only Clary's emergence from the exam room saved her from bursting into tears.

He was dressed, but haphazardly, his shirt hanging out over pants that rode low on his hips and bagged behind. She went to him, put a hand gingerly around his waist so as not to hurt the bruises that made it too painful for him to fasten his pants. He slung an arm around her shoulders, and Ellie told herself it felt so natural only because they'd found themselves in this position before.

"I can drive," he insisted when they made it the two blocks to where he'd left his truck and she tried to steer him toward the passenger side.

"No, I'm driving. Doc said your reflexes are bound to be sluggish, so unless you want to cause an accident on the way to your apartment…"

She didn't need to finish the sentence. The truck was still parked in the street, and several irate drivers were milling around on the sidewalk. Whether it was the audience or common sense, he let her help him into the passenger side. Adjusting the seat to suit her much shorter stature was more problematic. It would have taken two of them to move the heavy bench, and although Clary didn't make a sound, the beads of sweat popping out on his upper lip when he tried to bump them forward had Ellie scooting toward the steering wheel instead. She could reach the pedals, but she had almost no leverage with the seat back a good foot behind her. The fact that Clary didn't object to her driving in such an unsafe manner indicated to her how bad he felt.

Pain, however, hadn't damaged his powers of observation one bit. "So, what was that between you and Doc?"

"We were talking about you." Not a lie, exactly. They had been discussing him at one point. "Doc said you're just bruised, but you're going to be sore and stiff."

"I already am. By the time tomorrow rolls around—"

"You'll be miserable," Ellie finished for him. "I'm sorry, Clary."

"You aren't blaming yourself for this."

"You got a concussion because I had a conversation with Lem Darby." She pulled up in front of the sheriff's office and got out, joining him by the passenger side. "Now you've been hit by a car because I said the wrong thing to a teenage girl."

"Okay, looked at in that light, I can see how you might think I would blame you."

"You're not?" she asked as she eased her arm around his waist and he draped his over her shoulders as they'd done at the clinic. "Because, personally, I'm blaming me."

He shushed her by putting his fingers over her lips.

Ellie went completely still, all but her eyes, which lifted to his. Their gazes held for a long moment, the warmth of Clary's touch seeping into her heart. She stepped back, away from the arm lying so comfortably on her shoulder, away from the fingers on her tingling lips, and if he fell down, oh well. Any additional bruises Clary incurred would heal a lot more quickly than her heart if she foolishly lost it to a man who'd never love her back.

"It's not your fault."

"You should get inside and rest." She walked beside him as he navigated the steps up to the front door. She didn't touch him.

"You couldn't have known how the people in this town would react," he continued. "I only blamed you because you were new, and because I needed a reason to keep you—"

"Don't."

If she'd shouted it, that single word wouldn't have had more effect than the quiet, strained way she said it.

"Ellie—"

"Let's just get you upstairs," she said, steeling herself before she put her arm around him again. Touching him meant facing what it did to her, but it also meant she could get away sooner—run away, she amended, when lying to herself didn't sit well. She could run away and hide. She could tell herself that whatever went on inside her when she touched Clary was something she could ignore. And she could pretend to believe it.

She'd expected him to object that he wasn't an invalid; he didn't. He could have made it up the narrow stairway by bracing his hands on both walls, but he leaned on her. The possibility that he might be looking for excuses to keep her close was more frightening than anything else.

"Do you want something to eat?" she asked, when they'd made it to his apartment and she could get some distance.

"Edie makes deliveries when the diner isn't busy. I'll call and have her bring something over later."

The sting of jealousy confirmed it, the idea of Edie coming up to his small, cozy loft… Ellie was definitely falling in love with Clary, but it wasn't too late to put a stop to it.

"Take one of those codeine-laced pills Doc gave you

and get some rest," she said. "It's the best thing for the bruises."

"Fine," he said, but he didn't move from in front of the stairway so she could leave.

"I have to go."

He caught her arm as she tried to walk by him. He held her loosely, but she found herself too weak to even try to break his grip.

"You should stay away from me," she managed to say.

"Because I've had a couple of accidents when you were around?" His smile faded when she only shook her head. "There's something else bothering you."

"At the moment it's you. It would be a mistake for us to get involved."

"Why?"

"Because I work eighteen hours a day, and I have a teenage brother—"

"Who seems to be doing very well. There hasn't been any more trouble at school, right? And he's obviously enjoying working with Sam. He spends all his spare time doing it."

"Which allows him to avoid this town and everyone in it. He'll never adjust as long as he can escape. And when I'm not worrying about him I'm worrying about my patients."

"Why?"

She might've known he'd home in on that. "I used to be a psychiatrist," she hedged. "Getting up to speed as a medical practitioner again takes most of the energy I have, and Luke takes the rest. There's no room in my life for anything or anyone else. Please, leave me alone."

"No."

Ellie closed her eyes, fighting off tears of frustration and loss. "I'm sure we'll be seeing each other around town," she said when she felt steady enough, "and we'll probably have to work together whenever there's an emergency. Otherwise you can consider me just another citizen of Erskine."

Clary seemed to get some amusement out of that, judging by the way his eyes sparkled. "I suppose it would be wrong of me to do this to one of my citizens," he said, pulling the scarf from her hair. "And if I did this," he leaned in to kiss her on the neck, "I'd probably get in real trouble."

Ellie was already in trouble. She tried to retreat, but he'd herded her into a corner, and not just physically.

He gathered her into his arms and she let him. They didn't have a future, but she decided to give herself this one kiss. She curled her arms around his neck and simply enjoyed the feel of his body against hers, the gentleness of his hold, the slow and thorough way he kissed her, as if it was the most important thing he'd ever do in his life, and he wanted to be sure he did it right. And, boy, did he do it right. There was respect in Clary's kiss, and yet he left her no doubt that he wanted her in every way a man wanted a woman.

He dropped his mouth from hers, dragged it along the edge of her jaw to her ear, whispering, "Stop me."

THE SOUND OF A TRUCK pulling into her driveway stole Ellie's attention from the mountain of charts on the kitchen table, and took her to the front door. She half expected to see Clary's white Blazer with the sheriff's shield on the door. Knowing him, he wouldn't take the painkillers Doc Tyler had prescribed, just in case somebody's cat went up a tree and he had to rescue it.

The man had been hit by a car and still he asked her to stay the night. And if it hadn't been for Luke, she wasn't sure she'd have had the strength to refuse him. Of course, nothing would've happened, at least nothing physical, but it was the emotional stuff she had to worry about, anyway.

Instead of Clary, however, it was Sam Tucker climbing out of the dusty red F-150 parked in her driveway. Luke opened the passenger side door, then took a couple of minutes to get all his stuff together.

A whole gamut of emotions flashed through her, not the least of which was disappointment, but when she smiled, it was genuine and welcoming.

Sam climbed the porch stairs, his eyes on her face the whole time. "You look happy to see me. And relieved. Let me guess, something to do with Clary?"

"Who's the psychiatrist around here?" she joked, but her eyes filled with tears.

"What did he do now?"

She knew Sam wasn't referring to the accident, he couldn't possibly have heard about it since he'd been out of town working. But hearing Clary's name brought it crashing back. "You must think I'm a basket case, Sam," she said, wiping her cheeks and getting hold of herself so she could give him a stripped-down version of what had happened in town. "He's bruised up pretty badly," she finished, "but he's fine."

"And you're not. I guess that means there's no hope for me."

Luke came up the stairs behind Sam, putting an end to that subject, to Ellie's relief. "Did you guys have dinner?" she asked, making sure her upset didn't show.

"Yeah," Luke said, brushing by her. He stopped at the doorway. "Thanks for asking," he said, without a hint of sarcasm in his voice.

Astonished, Ellie watched him go inside. When she

looked at Sam, he answered her unspoken question with a negligent shrug.

"Luke's a smart kid," he said. "It was just a matter of time before he stopped wasting his energy being mad at you."

It sounded plausible; Luke was a smart kid, but Ellie figured Sam had probably had a hand in Luke's transformation.

"You want to come in? Have a beer?"

"I should be getting home," Sam said. "How about a rain check? Or better yet, let's hit the Ersk Inn one night this week. See if we can't get the deputy sheriff's boxers in a bunch."

Ellie wanted nothing to do with Clary's boxers—at least, it was an urge she had every intention of resisting.

"Anything to eat around this joint?" Luke yelled from inside the screen door.

"I thought you said you'd already had dinner."

"Yeah, but that was two hours ago."

Ellie laughed, really laughed for what felt like the first time in ages. "Thanks, Sam. For everything."

"I should be thanking you," Sam said. "I put in fifteen-hour days this time of year, and Luke works right alongside me. I won't say having him there cut my workload in half, but I'm way ahead of schedule. I'm not making allowances for him being a city kid, either." He looked past her, into the house where they could hear Luke banging around in what was left of the kitchen. "Kid never complains."

Ellie crossed her arms.

Sam mimicked her stance, right up to the raised eyebrow. "That's my story."

"Sure, you men always stick together."

Sam's smile lost some of its openness. "Ellie, about Clary…" He hesitated, clearly waging some sort of internal battle. "All kidding aside," he finally said, "if you ever need a friendly shoulder, Luke knows where to find me."

"In this town everyone knows where to find everyone."

"Hell," Sam said, "in this town, I'll probably know you need me before you do." Before she could think of a response, his long legs took him to the truck. "I'll be over by Plains City tomorrow, so tell Luke I'll pick him up from school, and Ellie? I'll stop in and check on Clary."

"I seem to always be thanking you, Sam."

"Part of my master plan to win you over." He winked at her. "Otherwise Clary will never let me hear the end of it."

Chapter Eleven

A week and a half later Ellie stood in front of Janey and Noah Bryant's grand old Victorian in the soft evening twilight, her hand resting on the wrought-iron gate. She'd been invited for dinner, and she'd accepted—partly out of curiosity, if she was going to be completely honest with herself. She wanted to know what kind of woman Clary had been in love with, and the one short appointment she'd had with Janey hadn't told her much. A woman who'd just been informed she was pregnant wasn't exactly acting like herself. Mostly, though, Ellie was tired of her own company, and this was the one place she knew she wouldn't run into Clary.

Since he'd kissed her, she'd stayed out of town as much as possible, taking home visits instead of clinic hours, and rounds at the nearest hospital, an hour away, in Plains City. It meant longer days, but she really hadn't wanted to risk running into Clary after she'd run out on him. She'd let him stir her up, she'd done some stirring of her own, and when he wanted to go down the path she'd led him, she'd bolted. It had been the best decision, in light of Clary's injuries.

But they both knew that wasn't Ellie's real reason for running away.

"Are you coming in, or does that wine need to age a while longer?"

Ellie looked up and saw Janey Bryant standing in the rectangle of light that was her open front door, the smile on her face taking the sting out of the sarcasm.

"It's sparkling grape juice." Ellie pushed through the gate and climbed the steps, holding the bottle out as she reached the top.

"That was thoughtful of you."

"It was self-defense. If it had been alcoholic, it might not have made the trip intact."

Janey looked from the bottle to Ellie. "You're nervous? About having dinner with us?"

"I was nervous about walking through town. There's no such thing as off-duty for a doctor around here, and no telling… Let's say I've heard some unique stories over the past few weeks."

"Now you know why Doc Tyler begged you to move here. If you're feeling this way after less than a month, can you imagine how tired you'd be after forty years of listening to Erskine's problems?"

"Believe it or not, I like this place."

"You won't feel that way when winter hits," Janey predicted, leading the way inside.

Ellie stepped into the entryway, taking a moment to appreciate the front hall with its gleaming hardwood floor, beaded wainscoting and wide crown moldings. She peeked into one of the twin parlors to either side and found a charming clutter of furniture, framed photos and comfortably worn upholstery and rugs. "Your home is beautiful. I thought of doing something similar with my house, but it didn't fit."

"No, Victorian wouldn't be right for the old Mason place."

Ellie could hardly hope to achieve the feel of a space that had been lived in and loved by one family for generations. She'd occupied dorm rooms and apartments, but none of them had really been home because home was the place she'd grown up and felt safe, and that, she'd always believed, had been taken away with her parents.

She was coming to understand, though, that home was where and what you made it.

"I didn't mean to criticize," Janey said.

Ellie realized her silence had given the wrong impression. "I didn't take it that way. It's only that I'm new at remodeling, and not very confident in some of my decisions."

"From what I hear, you've made a good start."

"You've been talking to Sam."

"No."

"Ted?"

Janey shook her head, stepping toward one of the parlors.

Ellie followed her, coming to a stop in the doorway, so she could take her time scanning the room. She got no further than the pretty scrollback settee to the left of the fireplace—and the man seated on it.

Clary rose, folded his hands, unfolded them, then stuffed them into the pockets of his jeans. He didn't meet her eyes, which was fine because she was busy glaring at Janey.

Janey grinned unrepentantly back.

It occurred to Ellie that the best way to make her point would be to walk out the door. If it had been just the three of them, she might've had the bad manners to do it. But

Noah made his appearance from somewhere upstairs, and she resigned herself to at least waiting until they'd been introduced before she offered some excuse and left.

Noah, however, could have cared less for manners and introductions. He went straight to his wife and gave her the kind of kiss that sent Ellie's already overstrung nerves singing like a power line in an electrical storm. She didn't dare glance at Clary with all the heat coming from the Bryants.

"I'd tell you to get a room, but it appears you have about fifteen of them handy and you still chose this one," she said.

Noah surfaced. "We've christened the other fourteen already. Oddly enough, we missed this one somehow."

"I'll be sure to note on both your medical charts that you have a healthy sex life. Or at least one with a lot of variety."

"Don't bother," Clary said. "This demonstration is for my sake."

"Really?" Ellie said to him. "Do you mean to tell me that Noah is staking his claim, so to speak?"

"Yep."

"Interesting. That's a very primitive response for someone who seems to be so civilized otherwise."

"Are you two having fun?" Noah said.

"Not as much as you were," Clary replied, his gaze going to Ellie, "but I'm working on it."

"Now that's what I call interesting," Janey said.

"In my profession it's called delusional."

"I think I'm going to like you." Noah linked his arm with Ellie's and escorted her into the kitchen. "You don't mind if we eat in here, do you?" he asked, voice low. "Janey's feeling kind of run-down, and I thought it would be easier for her than lugging everything into the dining room."

"You could do the lugging," Ellie suggested.

"True, but her pride's involved—"

"What are you two whispering about?"

"Noah's just taking me to see the kitchen."

"It's a mess," Janey protested.

"At least it has walls. Ted Delancey tore mine out. He keeps promising to put them back, but I'm not sure I believe him anymore." Ellie turned a slow circle so she could see the entire room. It was a typical Victorian-era kitchen, huge and spacious, with a big pine table in the center and a pantry off to one side. Homey and welcoming. "Since I'm here, is there anything I can do to help?"

"Sure." Janey handed her a linen-covered bowl, giving in to the inevitable when the guys insisted on helping as well.

Noah followed Ellie into the dining room.

"I know you thought the kitchen would be better," she began.

"This way Janey gets to throw her dinner party the way she wanted," Noah said, "and we can do the heavy lifting."

"They're whispering again," Clary called out to Janey.

"Noah's probably asking her to divulge confidential medical information regarding my health."

"And I was assuring him that fatigue is one of the side effects of a perfectly normal pregnancy."

"So is hunger." Janey took her seat and started passing dishes around.

"Your daughter's not having dinner with us?" Ellie asked. "Everyone in town says she's quite a character. I was looking forward to meeting her."

"She's spending the weekend with Max and Sara Devlin."

"Helping with the spring roundup, like she does every year," Clary added.

Ellie had done a pretty good job of ignoring Clary's presence up to that point, but suddenly she was all too aware of him, sitting just around the corner of the table. She tried to eat, but his deep voice filled the room, recounting stories of fishing trips with Jessie, complimenting Janey on the meal, talking easily about the town and the people in it. When Noah brought up the new Internet business he was starting in order to promote tourism and commerce in Erskine, Clary seemed genuinely interested.

"Maybe you could write an advice column, Ellie," Noah said. "People could send questions and you could answer them, maybe insert a bit of Western philosophy."

"I'm from Los Angeles. The only philosophy there is superficiality. Anyway, I don't have any spare time."

"I'm talking light-hearted," Noah said. "You know, a shrink with a sense of humor."

"And if the person who asked the question doesn't know I'm joking? There are a lot of troubled people out there. It would be wrong, and potentially harmful, to use someone's pain for entertainment."

The room grew very quiet. Not even the clink of cutlery on stoneware refuted Ellie's quiet statement.

"I'm sorry, Noah," she said. "I know you didn't mean it like that."

"No, but I didn't think it through, either," he said. "I guess you should stick with analyzing the people around here. Right, Clary?"

"Maybe you should start with Noah," Clary said to Ellie. "A man with his sense of humor probably has some issues."

"What about a man with no sense of humor?"

"I have a sense of humor," Clary said. "You'd know that if you ever said anything funny."

Noah opened his mouth, but Janey whacked him with the back of her hand. "You promised to play nice tonight."

Eyes sparkling, Noah leaned over to drop a soft kiss on her mouth. "I thought you meant after dinner."

"Hush!"

Noah laughed, rubbing his arm. "The honeymoon's not over yet."

"I'll let you know when it is." Janey's blush deepened, but she swooped in to collect another kiss, and this time it lingered.

Ellie looked away and caught Clary watching her. She held his gaze. She wasn't uncomfortable with Janey and Noah's display, and if it made her feel lonely, she'd already made it clear to him that she intended to remain alone.

"And speaking of honeymoons," Noah said, oblivious to the other undercurrents in the room, "what's the deal with Edie and Lem? Are they actually a couple?"

"Lem painted the trim on the town hall last weekend—"

"That was part of his community service," Clary put in.

"Okay, but Edie doesn't have community service. Maisie Cunningham worked the inn last Saturday afternoon, and she claimed Edie was in the town square every time she looked out the front door." Janey paused to take a sip from her wine. "Unless Edie has suddenly developed a strong sense of civic duty, Lem was her reason for being there."

And since it was gossip, Clary put little or no stock in it. "Business must've been pretty slow if Maisie had time to keep tabs on who was coming and going in the town square."

"I heard they were dating, and before you ask," Janey said to Clary, "it's common knowledge, which you would've known if you hadn't locked yourself inside your office the last few days."

Clary swallowed back the defense that sprang to the tip of his tongue. His silence earned him a puzzled look from Janey, but there was no reason to upset Ellie by mentioning the bumps and bruises that had taken him off his feet only hours after he'd gotten back on them again.

"I had lunch at the diner today," Noah said into the silence. "Edie's definitely a changed woman. That must've been some conversation you had with her, Ellie."

"Edie made the changes herself. I only gave her a sounding board."

Janey laughed softly. "Now you sound like Clary. To hear him talk he's the laziest man in town, but if you ask anyone else, he's The Lone Ranger, Clarence Darrow and Mother Theresa rolled into one."

"The Lone Ranger?" Ellie mused.

"Whenever there's trouble, who rides in to save the day?"

"That's part of the job," Clary said. "And a little of Clarence Darrow comes along with it, too, but Mother Theresa?"

"Oh, please," Janey scoffed. "When was the last time you took a day off, Clary?"

"It's hardly a difficult job. Most days I just wander around with nothing to do."

"Who checks old Mrs. Barnett's locks every night so she can rest easy? Who gets cats out of trees and bats out of the town hall and keeps every kid in Erskine out of trouble? And even if someone does get in trouble, you do what the law dictates, then find a way to make it work out for the best. You don't realize half of what you mean to this town and neither does anyone else."

Clary rubbed at the back of his neck, trying to will the heat out of his cheeks. Ellie was watching him with a mixture of amusement and consideration that only notched up his embarrassment.

"You're completely taken for granted, Clary. Anytime there's a problem, you get a call, never mind if it has something to do with your job or not. And you pitch in with no complaint," she continued over Clary's attempts to do exactly that. "Two days ago, for instance, Mr. Winston's cattle got into the road again. His cattle are always getting into the road, but does he mend his fence?"

"He's an old man," Clary pointed out.

"An old man who has you at his beck and call." Janey turned back to Ellie. "Clary raced out there because he was afraid someone would get hurt, and what do you think happened?" She waited a beat. "Clary got hurt."

"What?" Ellie braced herself, one hand on the table, the other clutching Clary's arm. "You were injured?"

"It was just a close call," he said. "Mr. Winston's bull is almost as old and blind and ornery as his owner. I must've chased him out of the road a dozen times with no problem, but for some reason this time he took offense to me waving my hat and yelling."

"He ran at Clary instead of away from him," Janey said.

"And Clary's a bit slow on his feet at the moment—" Noah began, only to be cut off.

"The day I can't outrun that old cuss is the day I turn in my badge."

"What were you doing running around with a bunch of cows, anyway?" Ellie demanded.

"It's my job."

"If you say that one more time, I swear I'll scream. It's not your job to herd cows, or babysit teenagers, or—"

"What am I supposed to do when someone comes to me with a problem? Tell them to go away?"

"That's what you expect me to do."

"That's different." Clary shoved his plate aside and slapped a brawny arm on the table, leaning forward. "I get paid—"

"You get paid to uphold the laws in this town," Ellie met him halfway, putting them almost nose-to-nose. "You do all that other stuff because you can't mind your own business."

"I do all that other stuff because it's my job."

She fisted both hands, making a sound that wasn't quite a scream, but managed to convey frustration, irritation and disgust loud enough to make Noah and Janey wince.

Clary didn't bat an eye. "It's up to me to keep the peace in this town, and I won't answer to you, or anyone else, about the way I do it."

"Fine." Ellie got up. "That's what we'll put on your gravestone. Here lies Deputy Sheriff Clarence Beeber. He did his job."

She turned to Janey, refusing to be embarrassed by the smug, knowing looks she and Noah were exchanging. "Thank you for a lovely dinner. We'll have to do this at my place next time." She leveled a killer look at Clary. "Too bad my table only seats three."

Clary, his expression as set and angry as hers, stood. "I'll walk you out."

He reached for her elbow, but she twisted away from him.

Janey and Noah rose, and she waved them back to

their seats. "You don't have to see me to the door. I know where it is."

"Sure you do," Noah said, "but we're not missing any of the drama."

Janey laughed, twining her hand with her husband's.

Another time, Ellie would have smiled, too. Janey and Noah Bryant were honest, fun, and so much in love it pleased her to be around them. They'd be good friends—as soon as they stopped trying to fix her up with Clary.

They all trooped to the front door, and after another round of farewells, Ellie found herself on the sidewalk headed toward her house on the other side of town. Clary was right behind her.

"You didn't drive?" he asked.

She refused to like the way his voice seemed to wrap around her in the dark. "It was too nice an evening to drive."

"It's bad enough you make that walk during the day, but at night? There's practically no shoulder, and every trucker from Idaho to North Dakota uses the stretch of the Interstate between your house and town and they don't exactly obey the posted limits."

"Maybe you should set up a speed trap."

"This isn't a joke, Ellie. It's dangerous. We have to go right by my place. I'll get my truck and take you home."

In her current frame of mind she didn't even want to agree with him on the fact that it was dark, but he wasn't going to leave her alone until he knew she'd be safe. "Sam said he'd be at the Ersk Inn if I wanted a ride home." Just to drive her point home, she crossed the street and headed for the inn.

"You'd rather ride with Sam than me?"

"At the moment, yes."

"What's going on between you two?"

"Why?" She whipped around, planted herself in front on him. "Because it's your job to know?"

"No." He took both her hands in his, his voice dropping in volume to a tone that tried to get under her skin. "But what if I want it to be my business, anyway?"

The anger drained out of her, so did the strength. It took every ounce of determination to draw her hands from his. "It's better for both of us if you don't mean that."

"You mean it's better for you, and to hell with how I feel."

She let that sink in for a minute, then decided she was glad he'd hurt her. It made her job so much easier. "You're right. It's better for me if you stay away."

"I'm sorry, Ellie, you're the least selfish person I've ever met."

"You're wrong about me." She walked away, chin high, eyes dry and burning.

"Ellie—"

"Stay away from me, Clary," she said without turning back. "Do us both a favor and stay away."

Chapter Twelve

"You could get arrested for that, whether or not you turn out your pockets."

Luke yelped and fell off the garbage can he'd been perched on, into a flower bed full of rosebushes. He looked up and said, "There's that Erskine cold shoulder again, biting me on the ass."

"More like putting you on it." Clary held out a hand.

Luke gave him a "back-off" glare, crawling carefully out of the rosebushes. "What are you doing here?" He got to his feet, trying not to make it obvious that he was checking himself over for thorns.

Clary had to fight back a laugh. "Mrs. Bessemer called me. Said the lunatic who tried to steal her bags a few weeks back was peeping in her windows."

"I wasn't peeping. I wanted to apologize and when she didn't come to the door…"

"You were concerned."

Luke shrugged. "That old lady could be dead in there and nobody would know it."

"I'd know," Clary said, and stepped up to bang a fist on the door and shout Mrs. Bessemer's name a couple of times.

"I'm outta here."

"Your conscience brought you this far, Luke. It's not going to shut up unless you see it through."

Luke rolled his eyes and huffed out a breath, but he stayed put.

A couple of minutes passed, and finally they heard some clattering from inside the house.

"Mrs. Bessemer? It's me, Clary."

The door opened a crack, and one beady eye peered out. "Did you arrest that crazy kid this time?"

"No, the crazy kid has something to say to you."

The door opened a touch wider, and Luke took an involuntary step back. "Does she always look like this?" he whispered.

Mrs. Bessemer's hair stuck out in every direction, her ratty-looking cardigan was buttoned wrong and she had on two different shoes.

"My grandmother never would've answered the door this way."

Clary figured they were lucky she was wearing more than her nightgown.

"If you have something to say to me, boy, speak up."

"I wasn't trying to steal your bags," Luke yelled. "I was trying to help you carry them. It was taking you, like, forever to cross the street."

"I don't need help," she blasted back at him. "I've been living by myself for eighty-five years."

"I can see why," Luke muttered.

Mrs. Bessemer got a funny little half smile on her face. Not so deaf after all, Clary realized. "You still want me to arrest him?" Clary bellowed at the top of his lungs, playing along with the old woman's game.

Mrs. Bessemer narrowed her eyes and glared down her

nose at Luke, quite a feat for someone who was barely five feet tall and so hunched over it was as if her head weighed too much for her neck to hold it up. "My rosebushes could use some trimming, especially the ones you flattened. Could be, if you came over another day, there'd be some lemonade and cookies around."

"Could be I'll be around another day," Luke said. And since he clearly didn't see any reason to hang out there now, he took off.

"He's a good kid," Clary said to Mrs. Bessemer.

"I can see that for myself. I'm not blind y'know."

"Only deaf."

She cackled out a laugh and slammed the door in his face.

"I KNOW MY WAY home," Luke said when Clary caught up with him.

"Don't want to be seen with me, huh? Seems to run in the family."

"I heard Ellie let you have it the other night."

"She told you about that?"

"It happened in front of the Ersk Inn," Luke reminded him.

Which meant that Luke and Ellie weren't talking about it, but the rest of the town was. Oh, well, Clary thought with a sigh, what else could he expect?

"How's she been?"

"Ask her yourself," Luke said. "She's supposed to be at the clinic today."

"I was by a little while ago. Her car's not there."

"If she's not making rounds or going to the hospital after, she walks into town," Luke said, and sure enough, while they were standing there Ellie appeared around the corner.

When she spotted them she came to a kind of jerky halt, lifted her chin, then put her feet in motion again.

Luke made a sharp right turn.

Clary nabbed him by the arm before he could step off the sidewalk. "Aren't you going to say hi to your sister?"

"She only gets that look on her face when she's about to ground me for something."

"She's not looking at you, she's looking at me."

"Yeah, well, the smart thing to do when she's in this kind of mood is stay out of her way." When Clary didn't budge, Luke added, "Don't say I didn't warn you." He took off in the general direction of the Five-And-Dime, or what Clary wanted to believe was step two on his journey of atonement.

Ellie bypassed Clary and put her key into the clinic door. She didn't acknowledge him.

"Luke apologized to Mrs. Bessemer this morning, and now he's on his way to the Five-And-Dime. At least that's the direction he's heading."

Ellie glanced after her brother, and Clary realized that, for all the apologizing Luke was doing, he hadn't made amends with his own sister.

"I have a lot of work to do before patients start arriving," she said.

Clary didn't take the hint, following her into the cool quiet of the waiting room.

"Is there something I can do for you, Sheriff?"

"You can stop being mad at me. I haven't done anything dangerous the whole week."

"In this town, just putting on that uniform is dangerous." Not to mention her white lab coat.

"Was that a joke?"

"Not from what I've seen." Ellie set her bag on the reception counter, turned and met his eyes. Whether or not she was ready, or wanted it, this man intrigued her on any number of levels, and the fact that he was a mistake she couldn't afford to make seemed inconsequential when she so needed someone to hold her.

After her conversation with her uncle she'd been determined things would be different. Better. All she had to do was visualize herself as the confident doctor she'd been once upon a time, and she'd be that person again, right? If you see it, you can be it. Basic psychology. It might actually have worked if the problem hadn't been compounded by absentmindedness.

She didn't blame Clary for the fact that she couldn't get him off her mind, though, she blamed herself. She was going about this thing the wrong way, she'd decided. She didn't need distance from him, she needed familiarity. If she saw Clary more frequently, it wouldn't feel like a big deal anymore, and eventually she'd stop thinking of him day and night. And if she stopped thinking of him day and night, she wouldn't be so...keyed up when she saw him.

"Maybe you should program my phone number into your cell phone so the next time you get injured you only have to punch a couple of buttons."

Clary stared at her for a beat. "I'm sorry, did you offer to give me your phone number? Not that I don't already have it—"

"You already know my phone number?"

"Doc Tyler gave it to me."

"Oh. That makes sense."

"No, it doesn't. Last week you told me to stay away from you."

Ellie wished she'd thought of this earlier. It was fun having Clary off balance for a change. "That wasn't very realistic, was it?"

"Uh…"

"I mean, this is a small town. You're the deputy sheriff, I'm a doctor, and considering how often people around here get hurt—you in particular—it doesn't seem reasonable to ask you to stay away from me. I wouldn't want you to feel like you couldn't call me if you needed to."

Clary tucked his thumbs into his belt and smiled. "So, if there's an accident, I should feel free to call you?"

"Sure."

"And say, someone is upset, not actually hurt, but just, you know—"

"Needs someone to talk to? You've got my number."

He moved a step closer, leaned in and dropped his voice to a suggestive rumble. "What if it's been a long, trying day, and I can't sleep? Should I give you a ring?"

She wanted to jump him, right then and there. But that would go away—eventually, right? "It's always nice to hear from a friend."

He winced. "A friend."

"Absolutely. If I can help you out in any way, Clary, give me a buzz and I'll do my best."

"Any way?"

She smiled blandly. "What are pals for?"

Clary stared at her a second with the pained expression of someone doing mental math and coming up with two plus two equals five. He appealed to the ceiling, heaved a sigh, and headed for the door.

All those times she'd told him to leave her alone, and

when she invited him to talk to her anytime, he walked away, dumbstruck.

Reverse psychology. Why hadn't she thought of that before?

CLARY SPENT the rest of his Saturday morning staring blankly at a stack of paperwork and stewing over Ellie Reed. For two months she'd been telling him to stay away from her. Suddenly it was "let's be friends," and "call me day or night.' If he was being honest with himself, it was the nights that kept grabbing his imagination and taking it on a walk through fantasyland. Not that his fantasies only revolved around the nighttime. He had some pretty wild ideas for her days, too, ideas involving breakfasts and lunches and dinners, laughter and conversation—which, when he got right down to it, was what Ellie had confined him to. Her offer was one of friendship, and that should've been fine with him.

He'd been comfortable with his existence, if not exactly happy. He'd known his place in the world, and he hadn't wanted more. Now, he felt things and wanted things that would only complicate his life in ways he didn't want his life to be complicated. He'd taken that road once, and it had led him to heartache and guilt and regret.

"Sheriff!"

Why did he hope that shout presaged some sort of crisis when he'd spent the last ten years working himself half to death to keep Erskine trouble free? Because he was tired of his mind running in circles and always coming back to Ellie. He wanted an excuse to see her. He got to his feet and went into the outer office, knowing it was a mighty sad commentary on his life when he looked forward to someone else's problem so he could promote his own agenda.

"Sheriff!" Babs O'Hara stood behind the long counter, all wide-eyed and agitated. "You have to come to the Five-And-Dime, right away."

"Calm down, Mrs. O'Hara, and tell me what's wrong."

"He's there again," she said, hands out, fingers splayed, breath coming in short, indignant puffs. "That Luke Reed. He came in a short time ago and said he was sorry about what happened before, and asked if there was anything he could do around the place to make up for it, you know, like community service, and I thought, well, there're piles of stock to be unpacked and Mort is off to some mule competition in Michigan. So I set the juvenile delinquent to unloading boxes and I put Lainie—you know, my oldest girl—to keeping an eye on him in case he gets sticky fingers again. Next thing I know Lainie says she's going to the Fourth of July dance with the kid!"

Babs stopped to suck in a breath and when she started babbling again, Clary tuned her out. He already had a pretty good grasp of the situation, and while she was taking it as some kind of personal attack, he didn't think that was the case. Sure, there might've been a bit of nose-thumbing on Luke's part, but Clary didn't believe he was doing it on purpose. More likely Lainie was the one making a statement, a bit of date-the-bad-boy-rebellion, considering how tight a rein her parents kept her on.

"Well, what are you going to do about it?" Babs demanded. "He's gone home now, but he'll be back, mark my words."

Clary didn't see how he could keep from marking her words, since they were loud enough to qualify as noise pollution. He braced his hands very carefully on the counter and said with a great deal of pleasure, "I'm going fishing."

"What?"

"It's been ages since I went fishing."

"But it's the middle of the afternoon."

"It's Saturday," Clary said. "I'm taking the afternoon off."

He never considered changing out of his uniform, but when the fax machine beeped and whirred into life, he paused at the door and almost went back inside. But that would've been a mistake. He'd decided to take the afternoon off, and by God he was doing it.

FROM TIME TO TIME, Erskine boasted its own newspaper, but each successive publisher learned the same lesson. By the time the paper hit the presses, it was old news. Erskine had its own way of disseminating information, and everyone in town was a reporter looking for the next big scoop.

Babs O'Hara got to be the woman of the moment, since she could report that not only had Dr. Reed's brother asked out her daughter, but Deputy Sheriff Beeber wasn't going to lift a finger to make sure the kid didn't steal something from Lainie that was more precious than a pack of gum. And what was more important than her daughter's ruin? Fishing.

By the time Clary parked his SUV in front of Janey Bryant's house, she'd already heard about his dereliction of duty. And Janey's daughter, Jessie, was already waiting out front with her pole and tackle.

"Opinion is running pretty much fifty-fifty," Janey said to Clary while they were waiting for Jessie to put her gear in the Blazer. "Half of Erskine thinks you're neglecting your duty, the other half thinks it's about time. And Jordy Fishman won the pool."

"There was a pool?"

"Not a very popular one. Nobody actually believed you'd take an afternoon off in the middle of the week. Mike Shasta tried to get some action on it by offering to double the payoff if there's a woman involved."

Clary didn't say anything but the tips of his ears started to burn. Thankfully his hat hid the telltale appendages.

"You're not going by Ellie's, are you?"

"I thought Luke might like to go fishing—and before you get on the telephone, I'm sure Dr. Reed is at the clinic today."

"I'm wounded you would think I'd do that."

"You weren't going to call Sara?"

"Well, sure, but I tell Sara everything."

It was unrealistic for Clary to think otherwise. The two had been best friends practically since the day Sara had moved from Boston to Erskine. "Go ahead and call her," he said, "but don't leave out the part where Dr. Reed is at the clinic this afternoon."

"What do you think the chances are of her being home when you drop Luke off?"

"I think the odds are pretty high that I won't make it an hour before somebody calls me."

"The odds go up if you shut off your phone."

"Can't. Something might happen."

"Yeah, Erskine is a hotbed of criminal activity." Janey plucked the cell phone from his belt, flipped it open and shut it off.

Clary held his hand out. She dropped the phone into it, but he didn't turn it back on. He weighed the potential consequences of his decision, then clipped the phone back on his belt.

"I could give Maryann a call at the clinic," Janey offered, "get her to reroute any emergency calls that are supposed to go Ellie's way. Then she'd surely be home when you dropped Luke off."

"Right, and Maryann wouldn't tell a soul."

"Just Doc—he'll have to go on call tonight."

"Thanks for the sentiment, but I'm already in enough trouble."

"Ellie doesn't seem like the kind of person who keeps score."

"No." Something else was holding her back. And Janey knew him way too well to miss how that bothered him.

She tipped her head to one side, giving him a funny little smile as she searched his eyes. "What's going on, Clary?"

"Nothing. Tell Noah I said hi."

"You coming?" Jessie shouted from the street.

Clary gave Janey a wave and headed down the stairs, chuckling because even at this distance he could see Jessie roll her eyes. "We have a stop to make," he said, sidetracking Jessie's protests by bringing up the obvious. "I hear you're going to be a big sister."

Jessie smiled broadly, telling him exactly how she felt about a new addition to her family.

"It's going to be different, not being an only child anymore, you know. You're going to have to share everything."

"It'll be at least three years before the kid can play with any of my stuff, and by then I'll be done with it," she said with perfect ten-year-old logic. "So where are we going?"

"How about we see if Luke Reed wants to go fishing with us. That okay with you?"

Jessie mulled it over for a second, then shrugged. "Been wanting to meet him, anyway."

Clary grinned as he pulled into Ellie's driveway. Before he could turn off the ignition, Luke came out to slouch against the front doorjamb, an insolent expression on his face.

"My sister's still at the clinic," he said when Clary and Jessie got out of the SUV.

"Didn't come to see her." Jessie skipped lightly up the porch steps. She stuck her hands in her pockets and stared up at Luke. "Why is your hair so long?" she asked. "You in a rock band or something?"

"Nope."

"I heard you had your eyebrow pierced."

"I do, but the principal won't let me wear it at school."

"Principals are like that," Jessie said. "Mrs. Erskine-Lippert's our principal. She looks like she's sucking on a pickle all the time, but she's not really as mean as she wants everybody to think. Why do you only wear black?"

"Why do you ask so many questions?"

"My mom says you don't learn anything unless you ask questions. But sometimes she gets tired of 'em, too. You want to come fishing with us?"

Luke eyed Clary's uniform. "Sure, hanging out with a cop and a kid will do wonders for my rep."

Instead of being offended, Jessie laughed. "Afraid I'll catch more fish than you? I can, y'know."

"I didn't exactly spend much of my spare time in L.A. fishing," Luke said, although Clary could tell from the way he shifted his feet that Jessie had found the right button. "There was actually other stuff to do besides going to school and watching the grass grow."

"It's not so bad here once you get used to it."

"Jessie's right," Clary added. "What you did today will

make it easier for you to fit in here, Luke, and I'm sure your sister will be proud of you when she hears about it. Mrs. Bessemer will tell everyone how you apologized, and Babs O'Hara, well, nobody really takes Babs seriously—"

"Is he always like this?" Luke asked Jessie. He shut the front door and came down the steps.

"No, usually he's pretty quiet." Jessie followed on Luke's heels. "I think he really wants you to like him."

"Uh, guys, I'm still here," Clary said.

"Like we could forget with you doing all that talking."

"Yeah," Jessie piped up, "you're going to scare the fish away."

"He has that effect on more than fish," Luke observed blandly, climbing into the back seat of Clary's SUV.

"If you're talking about Dr. Ellie, he doesn't seem to have much luck with women."

Jessie Bryant, ten going on thirty, Clary thought. "Speaking of luck with women," he said, eyeing Luke in the mirror, "I hear you're going out with Lainie O'Hara."

"What?" Jessie twisted around in her seat to gape at Luke. "Lainie O'Hara?" Clearly the idea of it brought her halfway back from the case of hero-worship she'd been developing. "She giggles all the time. Why are you going out with her?"

"She asked me," Luke said. When she continued to stare at him, he added, "I'm not going to, like, marry her or anything."

"I hope not." Jessie turned forward. "And what are you smiling at?" she asked Clary.

"He's smiling because he put me in the hotseat and you fell for it," Luke said.

"Not for long."

Clary reversed out of Ellie's driveway, exhaling heavily. "Let's not forget fishing is a quiet sport."

Chapter Thirteen

Ellie was working in the garden when Clary pulled up in front of her house.

He slammed the door of the Blazer, swearing as she started to drag a huge azalea bush toward the hole she'd dug. "You couldn't settle for annuals like a normal person?"

"Too polite."

He stomped over and lifted the bush with one hand, plunking it in the hole.

"Turn it... Yes, like that." She stood back so she could admire the way the outrageously deep pink blooms looked against the weathered wood of her porch.

Clary wasn't so bad to look at, either. She'd always been the kind of woman who went for brains and sensitivity in a man, but she had to admit there was something to be said for brawn. All those muscles bunching and flexing, and that sexy little grunt he'd made when he'd picked up the azalea. He took a shovel and bent forward to push dirt in the hole, giving her a view of a really good butt covered in uniform pants, whose starch was no match for his spectacular musculature.

"What's with the greenery?"

Ellie jerked around, surprised to find Luke standing behind her. "I thought you were with Sam," she said to him. And then she considered some of the reasons the deputy sheriff might be escorting her teenage brother home and the heat inside her changed from the kind she'd worked very hard to ignore to the kind she had no trouble indulging.

She slipped her hands onto her hips. "What's going on?"

"I took Jessie Bryant and Luke fishing."

"You went fishing?" she said to her brother. "Willingly?"

"Jeez," Luke said, "chill."

"Wait a second." She turned back to Clary. "Since when do you take time off?"

He looked up, and when his eyes met hers, she jolted. He held her gaze long enough to make her more than a bit unsure of her ability to keep things casual between them. And then Luke spoke and the spell was broken.

"Was Ted here today? What's happening with my room? Do I have actual walls yet?"

"Ted and his crew were here when I got home from the clinic," Ellie said. "They left a little while ago. I don't know what's going on with your room, but if you're hungry you'll have to make a sandwich. They haven't made any progress on the kitchen."

"I ate already." Luke climbed the steps and opened the screen door, pausing to explain, "Jessie's mom cooked us dinner. Phone's ringing," he added before he went in to answer it, leaving Ellie alone with Clary.

They stood there, Ellie's mind racing a mile a minute. *Walk over to the porch steps,* she told herself, *say thank you for bringing Luke home, turn around and go through the front door.* She followed her own advice, right up to the point where she thanked Clary, but instead of going inside she found herself asking, "Why did you take Luke fishing?"

"I thought he might want to do something besides work. He hasn't exactly been welcomed to Erskine with open arms."

"He hasn't exactly gone out of his way to fit in, either."

"True, but now that he's dating Babs O'Hara's daughter, things are bound to get even stickier for him."

"Back up a bit," Ellie said, forgetting about the still-un-imaginable happenstance of Clary taking time off. "Dating? What do you mean?"

"I mean that thing where a boy and a girl go out to dinner or a movie, or in Luke and Lainie O'Hara's case, the Fourth of July dance. If it's that foreign a concept to you, Ellie, I could show you how it works sometime."

She didn't know how to answer that, and luckily Clary didn't push the issue.

"How's it coming?" he asked, motioning toward the house.

"It seems they discovered some issues with the wiring once they got the walls out. You couldn't prove it by me, but Ted insists progress is being made."

"That was Sam on the phone," Luke said from inside the screen door. "Harv Purcell's mare is foaling."

"And you want to be there." She could hear it in his voice. "Why don't you take the car? Tomorrow's Sunday, so I'm not in the clinic, and I'm not on call. As long as you're back tomorrow night I'll be okay."

Luke opened his mouth, hesitated, then mumbled, "thanks," and disappeared into the depths of the house.

Ellie had seen the pleasure lighting his face, and the excitement. It didn't matter whether it had been over the horse foaling or getting to take the car because she was almost sure she'd seen a flash of warmth in his eyes. For her.

"What are you going to do with all that time on your hands?" Clary asked.

"Finish planting my azaleas, weed the flower beds," she said, putting that small kernel of happiness aside to savor later. "Everything needs trimming."

"It's supposed to rain tomorrow."

"Really? In the morning? Just drizzle or is it going to pour?"

Clary folded his arms on the porch railing, raising one eyebrow.

"How about the temperature? Are you predicting a warm, rainy Sunday or the kind that makes you want to wrap up with a blanket and a good book?"

"Having fun?"

"The digging was kind of entertaining, but talking about the weather... What could top that?"

"I could think of a couple things."

And if her imagination hadn't supplied them, the suggestive look on his face would have. Even if she'd pulled an Edie, she wouldn't have been able to find any words in her brain.

Luke shot out of the house, a black T-shirt straggling out of the half-zipped duffel in his hand. The screen door flapped shut behind him at the same time he jumped from the top step. "Hey, Buford, can you move your wheels?"

Ellie wouldn't have thought his appearance timely, if she hadn't noticed how hard he was working to ignore the tension between the two adults. The fact that he'd chosen to interrupt when she was obviously flustered pleased her, but she wasn't about to overlook his rudeness. "Luke—"

"He's talking about some movie called *Walking Tall,*" Clary said to her. "I gather Buford was a good guy."

"The Rock was Buford, and Buford kicked ass," Luke explained. "I'm putting the top down."

"It's supposed to rain tomorrow," Ellie warned, grinning when Clary stopped halfway to his SUV and looked back at her.

"I'll put it up when I get to Sam's."

"Okay," she said absently, her gaze still locked with Clary's.

"Uh, Clary? You taking off or what?"

He didn't say anything, only smiled, but it wasn't like any smile Ellie had seen before. Her heart leapt into her throat when she identified the new additive. Tenderness. There hadn't been any tenderness in her life in a long time, not since her parents died. It might be the one thing she couldn't resist. Thank God he was leaving, was all she could think. But he didn't leave, not entirely. He backed out of her driveway far enough to let Luke out then pulled in again.

Great. She had about two seconds to get herself together or he'd take one look at her and know he'd hit a weak spot. She went down the steps and started shoveling dirt around the azalea roots.

He took a seat on the top stair, and she could feel him watching her. The silence drew out and out, and although she knew it was a ploy on his part she felt a need to fill it. "Thank you for taking so much time with Luke," she said. "He's not the kid he used to be, but he's better."

"It would help if I understood what the problem is."

She picked up the watering can and poured a good amount in the half-filled hole. "Our parents died when he was ten. I'd recently started medical school, so he went to live with our grandmother."

"And you think you should've put your life on hold to raise him."

Ellie looked up at that, met his eyes. "I would have, but Grandmother insisted, and at the time…"

"You'd just lost your parents, too."

She glanced away. That was territory she didn't want to travel with Clary. "Grandmother died not long after I graduated from medical school, and Luke came to live with me, but, well, he's lost everyone in his life who mattered to him—"

"Except you."

"And I haven't taken the time with him that I should. Even when my internship and residency was done, a new doctor is always working or on call. I spent far more time with my patients than I did with him. He resents me for it."

"And for bringing him here."

"You noticed?" she said with a weak laugh. "Uncle Don needed us, and I thought it would be best to make the move now, before I got established in a practice or a hospital somewhere. I knew it would be difficult for Luke, but I never realized it would be this bad."

"Doc's no spring chicken," Clary said, "but he's not at death's door, either. You could always go back for a year so Luke could finish high school with his friends."

"No!" She'd said that way too hastily, and she didn't waste time hoping Clary hadn't noticed, only took a deep breath and acted as though it never happened. "We're here now, and Luke is finally beginning to make friends. And there's Sam."

"What about Sam?"

That brought her gaze to his, the glint in his eyes confirming what she'd heard in his voice. She almost justified his jealousy. It was tempting. But it was also wrong. Even if she would have stooped to using someone to make her life simpler, Sam and Clary were friends, and she wouldn't trample on that. "Luke hasn't said anything, but he loves working with Sam. You saw the way he raced out of here when Sam called." She leaned on the shovel, relaxing as the conversation turned onto a safer path again. "Besides, Uncle Don is our only relative. He needs us and I think it's good for both of them to spend some time together before Luke goes off to college and ends up who knows where."

"What about you? I don't hear anything about what's good for you. Didn't you leave anyone behind in Los Angeles?"

"I had friends," she said.

"Male friends?"

She started shoveling dirt again.

"Luke isn't the only one who's closed down," he said, coming over to her. "You're closed down, too, Ellie. Why is that?"

She tried to move past him, but he put a hand on her shoulder.

"I don't have time for this," she said.

Clary knew she wasn't talking about the conversation, and neither was he. "You could make the time."

"There are only twenty-four hours in a day, and right now I'm working about eighteen of them. So unless you can think of a way for me to give up sleep entirely, then, no, I can't make the time."

"I've given up sleep," Clary said, stepping closer so his body almost brushed hers. "You haunt me, Ellie, maybe because we have so much in common."

"The only thing we have in common is geography."

"You know that's not true." They both had shadows, different shadows no doubt, but he recognized them in her like he knew his own face in the mirror. He nearly asked her what troubled her so much that she would live her whole life around it, but dragging the truth out of her was the wrong way to go about getting it.

He could even let her go tonight, but he wanted her to have something to think about, something that would make it harder for her to hide from what was growing between them. He leaned forward and brushed his lips across hers. He'd intended it to be thought-provoking for her, but he hadn't counted on it stealing his thoughts, his breath. His strength. And he wasn't the only one.

"Are you done?" Ellie asked, pretending it hadn't affected her.

But he'd seen how her eyes had flown wide then drifted shut. He'd heard the beginning of a sigh before she choked it off. He'd felt her tremble and knew she'd have given in to what they both wanted—if she weren't so damn stubborn.

"No," he said, "I'm not nearly done with you. Or you with me."

"Then we're both in big trouble," she said, and kissed him back. There was nothing of patience in the way her mouth met his, nothing of restraint or control.

He swept her up, Rhett Butler-style, strode into the house, and when he was faced with empty rooms and nonexistent walls, snapped out, "Isn't there a bed in this place?"

Ellie buried her face in his neck, whispering, "Upstairs."

The fact that she was every bit as helpless against the intensity of this hunger only spurred Clary on more. He took the steps two at a time, bumping and banging against the walls.

"I'm glad that's not my head," she laughed.

"I'm sorry, Ellie." He let her feet swing down to the floor, but there was no getting a handle on his desire, not when she curled her hand around his, and pulled him down the hall and into a room with a bed.

He didn't realize it was the master bedroom, but he noticed the setting sun blazing through the wall of windows built into the new dormer. He liked what the golden light did to her skin, especially when he'd dispensed with her clothes and she stood in front of him, completely unafraid.

She should've been, was the only thought he had. If she'd had any idea how desperately he wanted her she'd have run in the other direction. But when she lifted her eyes to his, the vulnerability he saw there tempered his desire with tenderness. That didn't mean he was able to take it slow, only that he made sure he was very thorough, and that she found her pleasure before he even thought about satisfying his need. And afterward, he gathered her close and held her, his chin resting on top of her head.

Ellie lay there for a long while, enjoying the big solid bulk of Clary nestled around her. Until she caught herself drifting off to sleep. Sex with him was one thing, sleeping in his arms quite another, the difference between sating a physical need and a psychological one.

Yet she didn't have the strength to send him away.

Instead, she sat up next to him, pushing the rumpled mass of hair over her shoulders, then hugging her knees to her chest. She rested her cheek on one knee and allowed her eyes to roam over his body, laughing when he flushed.

"I've embarrassed you," she said, swirling her fingers through the light furring of hair on his chest.

"You're the one who's all folded up."

"It's not modesty," she said. "I'm holding the pleasure in."

His eyes darkened. "There's a place, right about here..." He skimmed his fingers from her knee to a spot high on the inside of her thigh. "That's the sound," he murmured as a moan caught helplessly in the back of her throat.

Ellie came up to her hands and knees beside him, dropping her mouth to the outer edge of his ear. "You're not going to stop there, are you?"

Before he could move, she slid her lips down the side of his neck and along his jaw until he caught her mouth with his, kissed her with the single-minded kind of concentration that she was only beginning to appreciate. But when he lifted, she shoved his shoulders back down on the bed and slipped her body over his. "It's my turn," she said, twining her fingers with his and staking them to the pillow. "I want to please you as much as you've pleased me."

Clary could've overpowered her at any time, but where would be the fun in that? Letting her have her way with him, now, that was fun. It was also an exercise in self-control that he nearly lost, but being helpless, under the right circumstances, was a completely new and liberating experience. And Ellie was definitely the right circumstances.

"I'm dead," he groaned after he'd had a chance to catch his breath. "I think you killed me."

"Don't even joke about that," Ellie said, and before Clary could stop her, she'd disentangled herself from his arms and padded down the hall to the bathroom.

Her reaction baffled him, and he followed her, reasoning that she would have closed the bathroom door if she'd meant to keep him out.

She was standing in front of a brand-new pedestal sink, staring into the mirror.

He positioned himself behind her, resting his hands on her shoulders. "What's wrong, Ellie?"

"My hair will be a rat's nest if I don't do something about it."

Clary reached around her and took the brush out of her hand, nudging her chin up until she was looking at him in the mirror. Their eyes met—hers dark, liquid, with a sorrow he didn't understand.

"You're wondering," she said softly. "Don't question this."

She turned to face him, her body fitting so perfectly against his it set off a dull ache in his chest.

"You wanted me here." She stroked her hands over his biceps. "And I wanted to be here. Isn't that enough?"

"For now," he murmured, dropping a kiss lightly on her lips. "But tomorrow—"

She quieted him by placing her fingers over his mouth. "We'll deal with tomorrow when it arrives."

"That's only reacting, Ellie."

"And you're a man who likes to plan ahead. I understand that. But life has a way of tossing unexpected little surprises in our paths, Clary, some of them unhappy."

"You can't see what your future will hold, but you can

buy insurance, save money, take precautions so that when those unhappy surprises come up, you're as ready as you can be."

"Yes, you can take precautions." Her eyes dropped from his for a moment, and she seemed to come to a decision before she met his gaze again. "As for the future, who knows if you can ever really be ready for it. By the time you get there, it just is." She smiled. "At the moment, I'd settle for a shower."

"I like you exactly the way you are," Clary said. He would've gathered her even closer if it had been possible.

"I've been working in the garden all afternoon."

"And I've been fishing with Jessie and Luke, and if you don't think that's work…"

She laughed, the kind of deep, full-body laugh that made him laugh right along with her. "Since one of them is my responsibility, I feel as if I should do something to make up for it."

"It was exhausting," Clary said. "I might not be able to make it back to town tonight."

"You could sleep in your truck."

He grinned sheepishly. "I'll probably be asleep by midnight, truth be told."

"Not if I have anything to say about it."

"You don't. This time I'm in control."

She looked over her shoulder at him, eyes hot with anticipation and bright with challenge. "Do you really think so?"

"Yeah." Never taking his gaze from hers, he gathered a handful of her hair and brought it to his face, drinking in the scent and feel of it against his skin. "If you give me any trouble, I'll have to break out the cuffs."

"Really?" Her lazy smile made his body tighten from toes to scalp. "How much trouble would it take, exactly?"

DESPITE THE LONG KISSES exchanged, the caresses lavished on one another and a leisurely lunch spent mostly in the bedroom, the last azalea finally dropped into its hole around midafternoon of the next day. Ellie showered, and then she made lemonade in an old-fashioned glass pitcher and poured it into glasses with flowers painted on them that she'd found in one of the kitchen cupboards when she'd moved in. By the time Clary was finished cleaning up, she was sitting on the back porch, bare feet propped up on the railing and her eyes on the orchard behind her house, each tree heavy with the tiny green nubs of apples.

Clary sat on the railing and pulled her feet into his lap.

"Mmm." Ellie let her head fall back, closed her eyes and savored the feel of his hands and what they were doing to her. He might be massaging her feet, but every muscle in her body went lax, and tremors raced through her, settling to throb deep and low.

She felt his hands slide beneath her and opened her eyes to see the world spin as he plucked her out of the chair, sat, and settled her back into his lap. Those magical hands kneaded at the small of her back. She rested her head against his shoulder and nuzzled her face into the crook of his neck. The scent of him, even mingled with her own soap and shampoo, curled through her, the first wisp of smoke before a fire ignites.

His pulse beat a frantic tattoo beneath her lips, his chest shuddered—and his stomach growled.

Ellie tilted her head back and found him looking down at her, laughter in his eyes, though the line of his mouth was tight.

"If you keep that up," he said, "I'll never get anything to eat."

"Are you really that hungry?" She peppered the short statement with kisses to his jaw.

"Starving," he said, taking her mouth in a deep kiss. "And I could use something to eat, too," he added with a smile that made Ellie's heart flip-flop in her chest. "We didn't eat lunch, remember?"

"Man doesn't live by bread alone," she quipped before she thought about what that old saying implied.

It wasn't lost on Clary, either, considering the way his arms tightened around her. Shock? she wondered, as she lost herself in the depths of his warm blue eyes. Or something else?

"I think we need to talk about what's going on between us," he said.

"Shh." She slipped from his lap, bending to drop a soft, fleeting kiss on his mouth. "You have this need to quantify things, Clary, to dissect and identify and place every situation into a nicely labeled box."

"And you don't." He caught one of her hands, studying the contrast of her small, pale fingers against his large, tanned ones. "It's early days yet. But the time will come when we have to decide what we want from each other. Where we're headed."

But not what we feel, Ellie thought, as she tugged on his hand till he rose and followed her into the house. And the fact that he'd spent an entire night and day with her, without once mentioning his job or the town had ominous implications. Clary was a man who made up his mind and then never changed it.

His heart, however, might be another story. No matter what he thought he was feeling for her, it wouldn't hold up to the secret she was keeping from him. Everything else aside, Clary was a man of high morals, a man who believed in justice. A man who'd already made it clear where he placed the blame when things went wrong.

"At the moment," she said with a forced lightness, "we're headed into the kitchen to fill your stomach."

"And after that there are one or two flat surfaces in this house we haven't christened—and quite a few vertical ones."

"I don't know, Clary... Luke will be home anytime."

"And you don't want him to find me here." His eyes shifted to hers, and he gave her a slight smile. "I agree, although probably not for the same reasons. Luke's not comfortable with either one of us right now. The last thing he needs is to feel like we're forming a unit with him on the outside."

"You're right." But that wasn't the reason she'd wanted him gone before her brother got home. Her reason was selfish. She didn't want Luke to know about her and Clary because she didn't need the guilt. Luke was finally coming around; she didn't think she could take it if he began to give her grief again. Not when the rest of her life, professional and personal, was on such shaky ground.

"Ellie?"

"Sorry, got lost in my thoughts for a minute."

"Feel like sharing?"

She opened the cupboards, finding them pretty close to bare. "Here I am in the middle of nowhere, looking for something to feed the deputy sheriff of Erskine, Montana. If anyone had asked me a year ago what I wanted out of life, this—" she gestured to the half-renovated kitchen, the wide-open land outside the window, and Clary "—wouldn't even have been on the list."

His eyes never wavered from hers, but she saw the curiosity come into them. Ellie realized she'd put herself in hot water, even before he asked the inevitable question.

"What did you want? Husband, family?"

"The name is Ellie Reed, not Donna," she said, even as she decided to stick with as much of the truth as she could. That had always been her philosophy and she wasn't about to change it now. "Of course I wanted to get married and have a family, but that was always somewhere down the road, after I got my career off the ground."

"Being a psychiatrist was that important to you?"

"Helping people—the ones who needed it the most—was."

It hurt. Remembering how deeply she'd wanted to help the lost, the misunderstood, those wandering in the maze of their own minds with no hope of finding the way out. And how easily she'd turned her back on that calling when it was convenient for her. "My life hasn't exactly gone the way I thought it would."

"Mine either. That doesn't mean we haven't ended up where we're supposed to be."

Ellie knew where he was going with that comment. She'd have headed him off if she'd had the least idea what to say.

"Do you think there might come a time when you could see us as a couple?"

"I see you as a man who likes peace in his own home, Clary, and we don't agree on anything."

"We got along fine last night."

She went to the mini-fridge and began to pull out the makings for sandwiches. "Sex is all well and good," she said, her voice casual, cool, "but it's not enough to build a successful relationship on."

"So you're saying there's nothing more between us but sex?"

"I don't think either of us is ready to commit to a lifetime. Let's just enjoy the moments we have for as long as it lasts."

"A lifetime is nothing more than a lot of moments stacked up on top of one another," he pointed out philosophically.

True, Ellie thought. She'd have to make very sure she didn't spend so many with Clary that they piled up on top of her until she couldn't get out.

Chapter Fourteen

Clary had been gone from town for a whole twenty-four hours and no one had missed him—and on a Saturday evening no less, the busiest time in Erskine. It was a source of some disgust for him to discover that Sam was right; Clary was overestimating his necessity to the town. He didn't waste his energy agonizing over it, though, considering the upside of the situation was that he got to spend some quality guilt-free time with Ellie.

For the first time since he'd returned to Erskine for good, Clary was living a fairly normal life spending his days in town, his nights at home, or the closest thing he had to a home. Ellie.

Now that school was out for the summer, Luke was over at Sam's almost constantly. Ellie clearly found his absence troubling, but Clary was only too happy to take her mind off the ongoing coolness of her relationship with Luke. Just another community service, he liked to joke to himself, but he knew differently. What he felt for Ellie wasn't going away any time soon. It probably never would. And although Ellie still acted like she could walk away whenever she chose, he knew better. She wasn't the kind of woman to give herself to a man without something more than sex driving her. Getting her to admit that, however, wasn't going to be easy.

Ellie studiously avoided any mention of commitment, even when it came to making plans for the next day. And since he didn't have a clue how to approach the matter of his feelings without sending her running, Clary took his cue from her. He always made sure to mention that he might be dropping by after Ted and his workmen went home, and he was careful to be up and gone before they arrived the next morning. Otherwise, the next couple of weeks passed in a pleasant haze.

They squabbled good-naturedly about what color to paint the dining room, or how long it would take Tom to finish the kitchen. And then they made up. A lot. Clary hadn't had a full night's sleep in days. He should've been exhausted; he was just the opposite.

The Fourth of July fell on a Monday, and it dawned a crisp, clear blue. Clary was up to see it, and to note that not a streak of color stained the eastern horizon. It was going to be a cloudless, sunny day. People would be coming into town early to stake out the best spots for the fireworks, so he'd made sure to be there before they started to arrive. But the memory of how Ellie had said goodbye, the way he'd slipped into her, all warm and sleepy, and loved her slowly awake, stayed with him the whole morning.

"That's some spring in your step," Maisie Cunningham called out as he threaded his way through the mass of people filling the boardwalks.

It was coming on noon, and the picnickers were leaving the baseball diamond and the sack races set up on the playground behind Erskine Elementary, and heading toward the town square and the coolers they'd left on tables or blankets in the shade.

"It's a beautiful day," Clary said, nodding hello to Arliss, her husband. Arliss was a man of many talents, being the town handyman, but few words, being married to Maisie, who probably didn't let him get a word in edgewise. "The sun's out, it's not too hot, and so far everyone's behaving."

"That must account for the smile you're wearing," Maisie observed with a grin of her own, just smug enough to give Clary a sinking feeling in the pit of his stomach.

He drew his face into a frown, then caught sight of himself in one of the shop windows. He looked like the theatrical mask of tragedy, so he toned it down.

Maisie's smirk, however, was perfectly executed. "Arliss came into town Saturday to help dig through that old storeroom over at the General Store. Hasn't been cleaned out in thirty years I bet, not since the last generation of Halliwells took over the place. Found some rare and interesting things, least that's how Arliss put it, right?"

Arliss grunted, Maisie continued. "Noah and Janey ought to drag some of the whatnot they found to that show where they price out antiques and doohickeys, see what they're worth. Some woman on there bought a table at a garage sale and raffled...no, *auction,* that's what they do, she auctioned it off for six figures. Can you imagine our Noah and Janey being on television and making all that money? 'Course, they'd have to split it with Mrs. Halliwell, that would only be fair..."

Clary would have made some comment to put a stop to Maisie's endless flow of chatter, but they'd left the boardwalk and were coming into the town square. It had been closed off to vehicle traffic, and with everyone in Erskine going in the same direction at the same time, he was completely walled in by people. Besides, as long as Maisie was talking about the price of antiques, he was safe from whatever she'd been working her way around to before. With any luck, she'd forget it altogether.

Or maybe not.

"...which is what I was talking about to begin with," he tuned in just in time to hear her say. "Before he went over to the General Store Saturday, Arliss had breakfast in the diner. He thought it was kind of odd that he didn't see you there, seeing as how you have breakfast there every morning, seven days a week, around 6:30 a.m. 'Cept for the last two weekends, that is."

On the weekends he had breakfast with Ellie, but when he had it with Ellie, it was a lot later than 6:30, and by the time they got around to food he'd worked up a hell of an appetite...which he shouldn't be thinking, Clary realized, glancing over to find Maisie and Arliss both watching him carefully. He wiped the smile off his face, but there wasn't much he could do about the color flooding it. "Hotter out here than I thought," he mumbled.

"Ain't it, though?" Maisie said, then snapped her fingers, curling her hand around Clary's arm as if she'd just had a brainstorm. "Y'know that might be why Dr. Reed's been so scarce in town lately. This heat's got her driving her nice, air-conditioned car. Used to be, when she first moved here, she wandered around a lot, heading to or from work or having her meals at the diner and such. Haven't seen the girl in quite some time and neither has anyone else—outside of the clinic, that is."

"Ted's working on her place," Clary said, in what he desperately hoped was a casual tone. "Maybe she's been tied up with that."

"Huh. Everyone knows Ted don't work on Sundays. Cold and flu season is over, too, so I'd wager she hasn't been called on her time off. I wonder what could be keeping the girl so busy," Maisie mused. "Maybe you know, Clary?"

"I don't make it my business to pry into the private affairs of the citizens around here."

Maisie completely missed the point, or chose not to get it, which was just as convenient for her. "I thought you were keeping an eye on Ellie, her causing so much trouble in your town. Or maybe that's why you've both been scarce the last couple of weekends. She's laying low so's not to cause any more trouble, and you're checking on her just to make sure?"

He looked over at Arliss, hoping to get some help. Arliss shook his head and gave him a look that said *Give it up, boy. You're no match for a woman on a fact-finding mission.*

Clary mumbled an excuse about being needed at the bandstand and made a quick left turn, to heck with the crowd hemming him in. He had to get away from Maisie before she wore him down and he stopped right in the middle of the town square and screamed that yes, he'd been sleeping with Ellie Reed. They had sex all night, every night, and during the day on the weekends, which would completely scandalize some of the people in town who believed sex was the reason God made it dark at night. And if daytime sex scandalized them, he could only imagine what they'd do if they knew about the whipped cream, or the apple orchard with its tall grass and cool shade, or the handcuffs—which suddenly seemed to be burning a hole in the small of his back where they were tucked into the waistband of his pants. Maisie was probably staring at them and wondering....

And he was being paranoid. There were dozens of people between him and where he'd left the Cunninghams, and none of them, including Maisie, were paying any attention to his handcuffs. To them it was just another part of the uniform, and although he'd never quite look at them the same way again, no one else had to know.

He looked up then, and caught sight of Ellie. And she caught sight of him.

The air between them seemed to ignite. By mutual, if unspoken, agreement, they both turned away before anyone noticed them staring at each other.

But that fleeting exchange lingered for Ellie, long after Clary had disappeared into the crowd. She had only to see him and she could feel the touch of his hands on her skin. His scent was as familiar as her own, the sound of his voice, the way humor blossomed on his face, as if pleasure wasn't truly pleasure unless he took his time about it. It was the little things that were so endearing... And it was foolish to let her mind wander beyond thoughts of him as a lover. Foolish and dangerous, she reminded herself, folding her hands in her lap so Edie and Lem wouldn't notice how they were shaking and ask her why.

At Edie's insistence, she was sitting with them at a picnic table dappled with shade from an oak tree nearby. Jessie Bryant had shown up to recruit Luke and Lainie O'Hara for her tug-of-war team and they hadn't come back for lunch yet. Sam had joined them for a time, before he spotted a potentially attractive girl and wandered over to see if, one, she was over twenty-one as that was his bottom end age cutoff, and two, if she was interested in a no-account rancher, as he put it.

It was just as well he'd gone. Sam would've expected conversation and Ellie was as preoccupied with Clary as Edie and Lem were with each other. Or so she'd thought.

"Who are you looking for?" Edie asked.

"No one," Ellie said, as she craned her neck, looking for a tall man with a head of sun-bleached hair.

"I figured it was Clary. Half the town thinks you're dating him."

"Where would they get an idea like that?"

Edie made a face. "It's partly my fault, I think. I mentioned that Clary hadn't come in for breakfast more than once or twice over the last couple of weeks."

"Who did you mention it to?"

"Well, nobody in particular, but the diner was kind of crowded at the time."

Ellie closed her eyes, but she couldn't shut out the truth. The whole town was talking about her and Clary. The last thing she wanted was for their relationship to come out. Having a romance in front of the entire town would be bad enough, a public breakup would be worse—no, Luke finding out she'd been hiding it from him would be the worst thing that could happen.

The next to the worst thing had already happened. She'd fallen in love with Clary.

NIGHT FELL, the fireworks went off without a hitch, and families made their weary way home. Big Ed's Rhythm Method, Erskine's one and only band, relinquished the bandstand to a kid from Plains City who wore his baseball cap sideways and called himself The CD Wrangler. He brought a vanload of equipment, tape decks, flashing lights, and the kind of music that sent most of the older citizens running for the hills. Even the country music selection was shockingly scarce on Hank Williams and Tammy Wynette.

That was fine with the cowboys who flooded into town, looking for action as the dancing began. The day had been torture for Clary, catching glimpses of Ellie and not being able to talk to her, touch her. Kiss her. But watching her in the arms of some random cowboy was hell.

Clary rested his folded arms on the railing of the raised bandstand, and from there he watched Ellie twirl around the floor in a lively two-step. Like everything else, her dancing was graceful and full of life, and she put every ounce of energy she had into it, her hair whipping around her in a silken cloak, long, bare legs a blur as her partner spun her in a trio of dizzying circles.

"I'll bet she's wondering why you haven't asked her to dance."

Clary never took his eyes off Ellie. Even if he hadn't seen Luke coming his way, he would have recognized his voice. "I'm on duty. What's your excuse?"

"Curfew. Lainie's mom made her go home. And I don't dance to this hick music anyway, but I bet you do, so why are you standing there when Ellie would rather be dancing with you than some dumb cowboy?"

"You a mind reader?"

"Don't have to be, and if you can't tell what she's thinking, you have no business sleeping with her."

That got his attention. "How'd you know?"

"Went into her bathroom looking for shampoo."

And he'd found the razor and toothbrush Clary had left in her medicine cabinet. Luke was smart enough to put two and two together.

"At least you're not denying it," Luke said.

"Why would I? I'm not ashamed of it. And neither is Ellie. She was concerned you'd be uncomfortable with her and me...that you'd feel we were...that you couldn't live with us as a couple."

"I think you need lessons in public speaking. And she needs to stop filtering everything through that psychobabble B.S."

"Yeah, it's not like you gave her any reason to think you'd blow a gasket if you found out we were...dating."

"You got me there."

"So can you handle it?"

Luke shrugged. "The question is, can you? She's not exactly the poster child for mental health— No, that didn't come out right. She's got issues, is what I'm trying to say."

"Everybody has issues."

"I thought you were Mr. Perfect. How else can you be so pigheaded about right and wrong if you're not?"

Clary chose to overlook the pigheaded part of that comment in favor of the bigger question. "I've made mistakes, like everybody else."

"What? You get caught shoplifting by that old sourpuss at the Five-And-Dime, or trash the market?"

"I let down someone I loved," he said, turning to face Luke, "and she died."

"Your wife got sick is what I heard. You think you could've changed that?"

"No, but I could've been there when she needed me instead of leaving her alone to suffer."

"So you drive yourself crazy making sure nothing happens to the people around here because you couldn't save your wife? That's as stupid as—that's stupid."

"That's human nature."

"You're punishing yourself for something you couldn't help and can't change."

It impressed Clary, how well Luke understood—maybe because he'd lived it. Only Luke wasn't punishing himself, he was punishing Ellie. And she was punishing herself because she couldn't fix things for Luke. "I lost my wife," Clary said. "You lost your parents and grandparents. But so did Ellie. She did what she thought was right for you, Luke. Bringing you here—"

"She came here for her own sake, not mine, and she doesn't care about anything but a bunch of strangers."

Clary let that hang, knowing Luke already regretted his outburst. And although he wanted to ask about Ellie, he thought it would be best to keep the focus on Luke. "How did you deal with your grief?"

Luke shrugged.

"Being angry, sullen, rebelling. Ring any bells?"

"Maybe." Luke looked away from the crowd circling the dance floor. "I'm just a kid you know."

Clary grinned. "Yeah, well, adults aren't that much better at figuring this stuff out than kids are. Do you think maybe Ellie's way of dealing with grief is to work herself to exhaustion so she won't have to feel it?"

"Sounds about right," Luke muttered.

"You've been pretty mad at her."

"Yeah," he said on a heavy sigh.

"It's gotten better since you started working with Sam," Clary said, "but you're not completely over it yet. You won't be until you can do more than say two words to Ellie and walk off before you have to see how much it hurts her."

Luke digested that as he stared out over the thinning crowd in the town square. "I guess I owe you an apology, too," he said after a minute. He reached for his right pocket, and Clary had an immediate flashback to that first day in the Five-And-Dime and Babs O'Hara's accusation of shoplifting. The hesitation in Luke's movement, the way his eyes shuttered were the same now as they had been then. And when he produced a picture, encased in plastic and attached to a keychain, Clary understood why.

"This is why you didn't want to empty your pockets in the Five-And-Dime," he said.

"My grandmother gave me this." Luke turned it over so Clary could see the photograph of a happy-looking family, a woman with dark hair and dark eyes so like Ellie's, a man smiling down at her. In front of them stood a teenage Ellie, and a kid of about five who had to be Luke.

"It's nothing to be ashamed of—"

"It's personal," Luke interrupted hotly.

"Yeah, it's personal, but it's not a weakness to love them. To miss them. Caring for people is a risk…" One he'd been afraid to take, Clary finished silently. He'd put his life on the line, but never his heart. Sure, he'd convinced himself he was in love with Janey Walters, but he'd known all along she didn't love him back so she'd been safe. And even though he'd pursued Ellie, he'd let her set the pace. Until now.

"Looks like I'm not the only one figuring stuff out," Luke said with the same kind of insight that came so naturally to Ellie.

"So, does that mean you're going to make peace with her?"

"It means I'm going to kick your butt if you hurt her," Luke said. His grin faded as he added, "She doesn't...she wouldn't..." He jammed his hands in his pockets and kicked at a clump of sod. "If she's sleeping with you it means something to her."

"Then why is she dancing with everyone else?"

"Maybe for the same reason you didn't ask her? So the freaks in this town don't make your life miserable gossiping about it?"

"Smart-aleck," Clary grumbled good-naturedly. That was part of it, sure, but not the entire reason they wanted to keep their relationship a secret from everyone.

Clary had faced what was holding him back. Ellie hadn't.

She seemed happy enough, but she was always just a little reserved, a little slow to smile. And there was such a surprised quality to her laughter—it was part of what made it so engaging, but it was also poignant. She'd had a lot of sorrow in her life, he knew that much, but if he had anything to say about it—

"You going to deal with that?"

For a second he thought Luke had somehow read his mind, then he picked the sound of raised voices out of the music and general crowd noise. He pushed off from the railing, scanning the horde of people until he located a cowboy on the far side of the dance floor, squaring off with Lem Darby.

Edie was standing nearby, both hands wrapped around Lem's arm, trying to pull him away. Lem wasn't budging.

"You owe Edie an apology," he said, and though his

voice was even and firm, his words rang loud in the sudden hush. "You don't talk like that to a lady."

"She's no lady. I wanna dance and I'm dancin' with Edie."

Clary made it halfway across the dance floor when he felt a hand come to rest on his arm. He didn't have to look down to know it belonged to Ellie. His body and heart told him that, just as he understood, without her saying a word, why she wanted him to let the confrontation play out.

Lem was going to face this sort of thing a lot if he intended to be with Edie on any kind of exclusive basis. She had dated a lot, after all. Not only would it take time for the word to spread that she wasn't available anymore, but some of the cowboys wouldn't believe it until it was proved. Lem was the one who needed to prove it, and there was no time like the present—though it was likely to be a painful demonstration, considering the cowboy had a few inches on Lem, not to mention the pounds to go along with those inches.

"C'mon, darlin'," the cowboy said. "You'n me both know he ain't man enough for you." He stepped forward, reaching for Edie, "and we already know I am."

Clary had to give Lem credit. He kept his cool, didn't rush to defend Edie, though it must have been killing him to let a comment like that pass. He placed himself in front of Edie, and when the cowboy made a lunge for her, Lem simply shifted them both out of his path.

The move was so smooth the cowboy found himself lurching into empty space, but the way he twisted and stared around, wondering where they went, was pretty comical. The laughter of the spectators, however, brought the blood to his face, and it wasn't all embarrassment.

He grabbed for Edie again, but this time when Lem tried

to shift away, he wasn't fooled. He gathered Lem up by his collar and drew his fist back.

Clary started toward him again, but this time it was Lem's voice that stopped him.

"You can punch me in the face," he said, shoving the other man's hand off his shirt, "and I'll sock you back, but all you're going to wind up with is a bloody nose or a black eye to go along with your hangover. No matter what happened in the past, Edie is my girl now, so you fellas are going to have to understand that she isn't available anymore. In fact," he looked over at her, "I mean to marry her, if she'll have me."

Edie shrieked, launching herself into Lem's arms, which resulted in the cowboy being shoved onto his butt in the middle of the dance floor, while Big Ed and company took over the bandstand to plunk out something that almost sounded like "Here Comes The Bride." The CD Wrangler might be good enough for the Fourth of July dance, but nobody was celebrating an Erskine engagement except Big Ed.

The cowboy climbed slowly to his feet, his face dark with anger and humiliation. Not only didn't he get the woman, he wound up on his backside, looking like a fool.

"Now you can step in," Ellie said as the man pushed up his sleeves and advanced on Lem. "Just be careful."

Clary, already a few steps away, paused long enough to give her a look over his shoulder, even if inside he was glowing over the fact that she was worried about him. It was rather anticlimactic after that. He caught the cowboy by the back of his collar and his belt, fast-stepping him off toward the sheriff's office. Behind him, the crowd closed in around Lem and Edie, congratulations and well-wishes all but drowning out Big Ed's halfhearted attempt to coax actual music out of three percussion instruments and one bass guitar.

"He's gonna lose his job if he don't show up for work tomorrow morning."

Clary turned his head and saw he was being followed by three other members of the same transient cowboy species that had spawned the drunk he now had by the arm. "He should've thought of that before he made a fool of himself," he grumbled, then considered what it would mean to his evening to have to babysit a drunk. "Give him a half hour and if he's cooled down and you're headed straight out of town, he's all yours. If not, your boss will be light one troublemaker."

He walked the man up the stairs and into his office, shoving him into a chair. "Sit there," he said, making a big show of rolling a police report into the typewriter. He could've saved himself the pretense. By the time he would have begun to type the pertinent information, the cowboy was already lolling half in, half out of the chair, snoring louder than a buzz saw biting into a green log.

Clary sat back in his chair and took a deep breath. It had been a hell of a day, so mentally exhausting that when he noticed the message light blinking on his answering machine he nearly put off listening to it until the next morning. He had twenty minutes or so to waste, though, so he plucked a perfectly sharpened pencil from the holder and pulled a sheet of scrap paper from the bin, then pushed the button.

"Clary," said the voice on the recording, a voice he instantly recognized from his army days. "It's me, Jack, you old stiff-necked son-of-a-jarhead. I sent you a fax a couple weeks ago, some pretty interesting info about your mystery woman. Kind of wondering why I didn't hear from you once you read it, then it occurred to me you might not have seen it at all. Wouldn't surprise me—never did trust those damn machines, anyway. Give me a call if you didn't get it. Hell, give me a call, anyway."

Clary sat there for a moment, staring at the silent machine. It should've been good to hear Jack's voice; they'd been pretty close friends back in their MP days. Suddenly, he wished he'd never heard of the guy, wished it with a violence that might have had him turning on a man who'd been his friend, just for being the messenger.

But that wouldn't change the message.

He turned, almost against his will, to look at the fax machine. At the piece of paper lying so innocently in the wire rack on its side. He remembered hearing the machine go off the day he'd taken Jessie and Luke fishing. He'd almost gone back to look at it, but ninety percent of what came through the thing was advertisements. The other ten percent were faxes he was waiting on, and he hadn't been expecting anything that day, or since.

He hadn't anticipated falling in love with Ellie, either, or getting so caught up in being with her that he wouldn't even notice a piece of paper lying on a fax machine, or remember that he'd called a friend in Los Angeles. But he had fallen in love and he'd let himself forget about the secret she kept from him. It had been a nice vacation from reality, and he'd believed, for a little while, that it could be a permanent state of being.

He'd been wrong. He retrieved the fax and laid it on his desk, read it, then sat back and waited for the other three cowboys to show up and haul off their drunk friend.

Chapter Fifteen

After Clary disappeared into his office with the peace-disturbing cowboy in tow, Ellie set out to walk the two miles to her house. Once Clary's official duties were fulfilled, he'd be heading to her place, and she had a scene to set.

It wasn't every day she told a man she was in love with him, and it hadn't been a simple decision to make. Holding back was killing her, though. She wasn't a woman who lied easily, and that was what she had to do, in every action, every time she and Clary were together. She hated always being on her guard, afraid she'd slip when they were making love and blurt out how she felt. Once, just once, she wanted to know what it would be like to simply give herself up to the man she loved.

And she wasn't about to let such a momentous occasion pass without some kind of fanfare. She went for the tried and true—candles, lots of them, and lingerie, short and black and transparent. There was food, too, cold fried chicken and potato salad she'd made with her own hands, after Edie had taught her how. She hadn't seen Clary eat all day, but she'd seen the way he'd looked at her before the dancing began. It would take only three words to have him looking at her that way again—

The front doorbell rang, startling Ellie out of her preoccupation—and puzzling her. She threw on a robe and went to the front door, but when she found Clary on the porch she was even more confused. He'd been coming in the back door as if he'd lived there his entire life and suddenly he knocked? And the look on his face...

"What's the matter?" she asked one hand lifting to gather the edges of her robe together in a futile attempt to ward off a chill that came from inside her.

"Can I come in?"

"Of course." She stepped back, closing the door after him.

He stood there, silent, turning his hat around by the brim. Ellie headed toward the kitchen, knowing he'd follow her, and that it was a shameless manipulation, but there was something drastically wrong and she needed every advantage she could get.

Clary, however, barely glanced at the table. He didn't sit, only stared, face expressionless, at a point over her head.

"I..." She swallowed, tried again. "Are you angry with me for dancing with other men tonight? I only did it to keep everyone in town from finding out about us."

His gaze flickered to her face, then away again. "Why don't you want anyone to know?"

"Because it's private, and because I..." *love you.* But the words wouldn't come out. The decision to bare her heart had been difficult enough to make, and that had been when she was almost completely sure he felt the same. This Clary... She didn't know this man, but she knew she didn't have the courage to put her heart into his hands. "You didn't ask me to dance, either," she said quietly. "Why not?"

"Because I didn't want to push you." He blazed up, all of a sudden. He got hold of himself almost immediately, but she could see it was an effort. "You're holding back, Ellie. I thought it was some sort of heartbreak in your past, something that kept you from giving me everything, like I—" He shook his head. "It's your past, but not a man you were involved with—at least not romantically."

He reached into his back pocket and pulled a rumpled paper out, dropping it on the table.

Ellie went even colder. "You checked up on me? Again?"

A muscle in his jaw tensed. "After we argued about Lem, Luke said something that got me to wondering."

"He was upset. You misunderstood—"

"Don't. Damn it, Ellie, you've been hiding something from me since the minute you got to town. You were furious when I only verified your medical license. With what Luke let slip, and the way you shut down any time I bring up your past..."

"You decided to go deeper."

"It's my job," he lashed out before she could put the hurt into words. "I have a friend on the force in L.A., so I sent him your particulars and asked him to see what he could find out."

She didn't bother reaching for the paper he'd dropped on the table. She already knew what it said. "How long have you known?"

"The fax came the day I took Luke and Jessie fishing. The day we..." He made a helpless gesture with his hands. "I heard the machine go off as I was leaving, but I didn't stop to read it, and then I forgot it was there. I found it when I took that cowboy to the office."

"Can I explain?"

"That's why I'm here."

She nodded once, then bent to blow out the candles. Her motions were jerky, every muscle in her body braced for the kind of blow she couldn't hope to defend herself against. She led him through the house and out onto the back porch. It was a good decision, she thought, as she took in the fresh night air and felt the queasiness in her stomach subside. The darkness suited her as well. She couldn't bear to see his face.

"I'd just started medical school when my parents died, and I buried myself in work. They sacrificed a lot to put me through college and I... It was silly, but I felt like I had to prove myself to them. I became absolutely driven, finished top of my class, did my internship at the biggest hospital in Los Angeles, and secured a place in a very successful practice. I was barely out of medical school and I had it all, the high-profile job I wanted, the friends, the house, the six-figure income—"

"You didn't go into psychiatry for the money."

"No." Ellie told herself she'd only imagined that his voice had warmed slightly. "I spent as much time as I could manage volunteering at the state mental hospital. State institutions are always in atrocious shape, never enough beds, and not nearly enough doctors for the patients they're forced to take in."

"And you met this..." she heard the rustle of paper and didn't need to look over to know he'd brought that damning fax outside with him "...Mathew Brody there."

Ellie closed her eyes against the sting of tears. It still hurt too much to put a name to her pain, but that didn't stop her from seeing his face. "He was so young, Clary, too young to be in a place where there's so little hope."

"You were pretty young yourself."

"Which is no excuse. Everyone told me he was a hopeless case, but I didn't know the meaning of the word *can't* in those days. I began working with him, and I was getting through. I know I was. If I'd only had more patience. I guess that's what comes from getting everything so fast. I was used to instant success. I was the fire-walker, the one who was going to reach the mind no one else could reach. And because I was so arrogant, I believed I was producing miracles.

"All I did was kill him."

"He took his own life, Ellie."

She rounded on him. "And who gave him the chance? Who gave him the pass no other doctor would give him? He begged and pleaded and promised me he'd be so much better for living like a normal person, even for one weekend."

"He must have been in a lot of pain, Ellie. And in the end, wasn't it his decision?"

"That was what my superiors said. Take some time off, learn from my mistake, remember Mathew the next time I thought I knew everything. The next time?"

"Ellie—"

She brushed his hand off. The last thing she could stand at the moment was sympathy. "I tried to do what they said. I took a couple weeks off and then I tried to go back to work. But I questioned every diagnosis after that. It got to where I was so worried about making another mistake that I couldn't function anymore. I took a leave from the practice, then I quit altogether. My colleagues knew, my friends… I had to get away."

"Run away, you mean."

"Call it whatever you want."

"I'm calling it what it is."

"It doesn't matter," Ellie said, suddenly weary beyond measure. "When Uncle Don called and asked us to come here it seemed like a prayer answered."

"So you convinced yourself Doc really was old and tired," Clary said gently, "and Luke would be better off in the country."

"I may have deluded myself somewhat where my uncle is concerned, but not my brother. Luke really was having problems in Los Angeles, and it's so much easier to get into trouble there. He's always had this goal to be a veterinarian, ever since he was little, so I hoped the country would be better for him."

"It is."

Ellie started at the sound of his deep voice. She'd gotten so caught up in the empty, directionless feel of that time that she'd forgotten she was no longer alone. "Uncle Don asked me to join his practice in a strictly medical capacity, and after what happened I thought it was best that way, too."

"And then I outed you in front of the whole town." He exhaled heavily. "Why didn't you trust me, Ellie? You should've told me the truth, especially once we were together."

"And what?" She demanded, angry that he could stand there and blame the whole mess on her. "You expect me to believe you'd want anything to do with a woman who was arrogant and stupid enough to cause a young man's death?"

Clary slammed the side of his fist into a post. "Do you think I'm that small-minded?"

"It was my fault Lem tore up the market. That was your take on things, Clary, not mine. And I was only trying to help, just like I was trying to help in L.A."

"That was self-defense, Ellie. The first time I saw you—"

"Don't." She turned away, but he pulled her back around to face him, taking her shoulders in his hands with an almost bruising grip.

"I was wrong," he ground out. "None of that was your fault."

"You're only saying that because—"

"Don't finish that statement," he said, so quietly she began to understand how deep his anger went. "Don't tell me what I feel or why I feel it when you can't even understand what's going on inside of you."

"I know exactly how I feel." Ellie shook his hands off. "And I know what went through your mind."

"You don't have a clue."

"Then tell me you don't see me differently now. Tell me you didn't read that fax and think I was responsible for somebody's death."

"I think you see everything through a haze of guilt and martyrdom," he said. "You might have left your old life behind, but you're the same woman you always were. An arrogant perfectionist who can't forgive herself for what she sees as a personal failure. Did it ever occur to you that in taking responsibility for what Mathew Brody did, you're making it all about you?"

"I'm not—"

"Yes, you are. Mathew's choice was made out of a pain no one but he could understand. And instead of trying to learn and grow from it so you can help others down the line and give his death some meaning, you chose to turn your back. You have a gift, Ellie, the drive to help people and the training to make it possible. Instead you ran away, not just from L.A., but from a job you were meant to do."

"This town doesn't need a psychiatrist."

"No, it needs a doctor, but you're not here to be a doctor. Are you any good to the patients you're seeing here, or are you afraid to put yourself on the line with them, too?"

"Is that Clary talking or the deputy sheriff?"

"I'm not sure you ever saw me as anything but the deputy sheriff."

She almost couldn't breathe. "I didn't sleep with the deputy sheriff."

"Then why didn't you let me in? Why are you hiding from everything—from yourself, from life? From me."

"I was afraid if you found out you wouldn't…"

"Wouldn't what? Forgive you? Love you? Do you think, after what my life has been, that I don't understand what you're going through? That I could hold it against you?"

Ellie fought for breath against the lead weight of pain bearing down on her chest. She'd known this moment was coming, but it was worse than she could ever have imagined. "I tried to tell you to stay away from me, but you wouldn't listen. I don't know where you thought we were going to wind up, Clary. I should've told you about my past, but even without that we're so different. I guess it's better you discovered the truth about me now, before…"

"Before I fell in love with you? That's not me talking, Ellie, that's you." Clary jammed his hat on his head and walked down the steps, turning to look up at her. "Let me know when you forgive yourself and you're ready to believe you're worth loving."

THE NEXT FEW DAYS PASSED in a haze of pain that gradually coalesced into a red-hot ball of anger until Ellie figured if Clary had the nerve to show his face at her door she'd show him what real violence looked like.

He didn't, of course. He was nothing if not a man of his word. He'd wait for her to come to him, and she'd be damned if she would.

Even if he was right.

He'd done a hell of a job psychoanalyzing her, she realized, when she could look back at that conversation with anything resembling an objective eye. He was absolutely on the money about everything he'd said about her. Damn it.

She supposed it was fate that his was the first face she saw as she rounded the last corner into town the following Monday. She changed direction, taking a deep fortifying breath when he did the same. He fell into step with her, neither of them saying a word, though Ellie made a point of keeping a safe distance between them. If he touched her, even by accident, she was afraid she'd throw herself in his arms and beg him to take her back. She couldn't do that, not and keep her pride. Heartache would fade in time. Even if it wasn't true she needed to believe it, and the occasion might very well come when she had to deal with him on a more personal basis than either of them might like. There were things that needed to be said so they could share the town and she could live her life without worrying about that day.

"Do you have a few minutes?" she asked quietly.

They'd made it to the town square by then. Clary

gestured to the huge gazebo that served as the bandstand, striking out across the grass toward it. Ellie followed. When they reached its shaded interior, she glanced at the benches ringing it, then decided she was too keyed up to sit.

Apparently, so was Clary. He took up his deputy sheriff stance, legs spread, arms crossed over his chest, but slipped off his hat and mirrored glasses, hanging the latter in the open collar of his shirt. She almost wished he'd kept them on; he looked as haggard as she felt, tired and unhappy and uncomfortable.

"You were right about me," she began abruptly, holding up a hand when his shoulders sagged in relief and he moved to touch her. "In refusing to acknowledge Mathew's role in what happened, I was making it about me. My guilt. My arrogance. My fear."

"I had no right to say those things to you, Ellie. I was angry—"

"Whether or not it was your place, somebody needed to say them. One of the first things I learned as a doctor was that I would lose patients. Maybe that was one of the reasons I went into psychiatry. There's so much less death to face. Or maybe my ego wouldn't let me believe it would ever happen to me. And when it did, I abandoned everything I believed, and everyone I might have helped. Including myself." She glanced up at him, but it was too painful to hold his gaze and say what needed to be said. "I was holding back, Clary, but not from you. I was holding back from me. What right did I have to be happy, to love and be loved, to have a family and all the things Mathew would never know? I was being a martyr. I was too close to see it."

It broke Clary's heart to see her eyes swimming with

tears, tears that he'd put there. Much as she'd needed to be kicked out of her self-imposed prison sentence, he hated to be the one who'd done this to her.

He took a step forward, but she retreated, such brittleness in her expression, in the way she held herself, that he knew she'd shatter if he made contact. A part of him wanted exactly that, to halt the flow of words that wounded him so deeply. But it would be wrong to stop her from saying the things she needed to say just to spare himself the pain of hearing it.

"The simple truth is that Mathew would probably have known little happiness, never mind marriage and children. That didn't make it okay for him to take his own life, but if he'd lived, I wouldn't have given those things up for myself out of guilt that he would never know them. Whether or not I managed to reach him, I would've come to accept that there was only so much I could do for him.

"I need to accept that now—I've begun to accept it."

"I'm glad, Ellie. If you knew how I've been worrying about you, kicking myself for hurting you like that." He began to pace, running a hand through his hair. "Can you…is there a chance we can start over?"

"No."

Clary stood there in disbelief as the happiness that had started to fill him died. When she turned away, he caught her arm and hauled her around to face him again. "No? That's all you're going to say?"

"I spent a lot of time thinking, Clary. At first I was angry, but when I was able to look at it objectively, I had to admit you were right about a lot of things. But not everything."

He closed his eyes, knowing what she was going to say before she said it.

"You told me you don't hold what happened to Mathew Brody against me."

"And you don't believe me."

She waved that off. "What matters is that you didn't know him."

"You're running again Ellie— No, that's not exactly right. You're pushing me away this time." He rubbed a hand over his face. "But it has the same effect. You still get to be alone and miserable."

"A martyr, you mean?"

"I was angry, Ellie, hurt that you didn't trust me, and I guess I wanted to hurt you, too. I didn't mean it."

"You can't just take it back." She whirled around to face him. "You have such a narrow opinion of right and wrong, I knew if I made the mistake of getting involved with you that way you'd break my—" She went over to the railing and leaned her hands on it.

She didn't have to finish the sentence. Clary knew she'd been intending to tell him something important that night. Candlelight, lingerie, the vulnerability in her dark, expressive eyes. He remembered the scene all too well now, but like the fool he was, he'd only been able to see his own hurt, then. If he'd held on to his anger, she would have told him everything, including, he believed, what was in her heart. "Anyone who really lives their life is going to make mistakes, Ellie. I did."

"And so will I." She faced him again. "I'm a doctor, Clary. One day something is bound to happen that's beyond my control, or perhaps I'll make a wrong decision."

"And someone will be hurt. Maybe die."

"You say that like it means nothing, but what if it's Sam?" she demanded, saddened to see his face go white, and to know she hadn't been wrong. "What if it's a child? Will you blame me?"

"No," he said.

"Now you're deluding yourself."

"So you're going to walk away from me? From us?"

"You already did that."

Those words, spoken with such gentle finality, hit Clary like blows. "I'm sorry, Ellie. Tell me how I can make up for it. I'll do anything."

"I wish things could've turned out differently, Clary, but I am who I am, and you are who you are, and we've just demonstrated that those two people don't belong together. I wanted to thank you, though. The last few weeks were wonderful, and now, well, you just forced me to see things in a new light, and for that I'm grateful."

"But there's no going back," he said flatly.

"It's going to take everything I have to go forward."

She looked so tired, as emotionally drained as he felt. Clary let her go; he could see that her mind was made up and she wasn't about to change it. No matter what he said. Or maybe it was cowardice talking; either way they were at an impasse.

Chapter Sixteen

"He's beautiful, Mrs. Hadley."

"Carrie."

"Carrie," Ellie repeated, gently tickling the latest generation of Hadleys, little six-month-old Nathan. "Everything is perfectly normal—better than normal. Nathan is in the 90th percentile for height and weight. He's on track to be as tall and handsome and athletic as that husband of yours."

Carrie blushed, catching Nathan's flailing baby hands in her own. "Thank you, Dr. Ellie, but I was wondering... Do you think Doc could take a look at him?"

"If you like." Ellie handed Carrie her blanket so she could wrap Nathan in it. "He's sleeping well, eating well?"

"Yes, but he cries sometimes and I can't get him to stop."

"He's your first baby, right?"

Carried nodded.

"And you're nervous. Babies are very sensitive. They take their cue from us."

"So it's my fault?" Carrie gathered her baby up from the exam table, his face clouding over as hers did.

"That's not what I'm saying," Ellie said before Carrie

could race into Doc's office. "I want you to try something for me." Nathan started to fuss, so Ellie took him from his mother and bounced him a bit. "The next time Nathan cries and won't stop I want you to put him down and take a minute to center yourself."

"A full minute? Should I time myself?"

Ellie smiled gently. "What's important is that you feel calm and confident when you pick him up again, however long that takes. And try to remember that crying isn't the worst thing for a baby. It's how they exercise their lungs. Now, I think Doc is free—"

Carrie reached out for Nathan, gurgling and happy again. "That's not necessary," she said. "Thank you, Dr. Ellie."

And that, Ellie thought, was advice that worked as well on adults as it did for babies. Taking time and centering herself was exactly what she intended to do. She saw the young mother out, leaning her elbows on the counter in front of Maryann's desk. "No more patients?" she asked, once Carrie had settled her bill and left the clinic.

"Nope. Doc is in his office, but he's probably napping. Old fool doesn't get enough sleep, if you ask me, and if you could make sure he gets a decent meal tonight, that would be good."

"Why don't you make sure he gets a decent meal, Maryann?"

"Oh… Well… That's not exactly part of my job description."

"But you want it to be." Ellie put a hand on the nurse's arm, stopping her midbluster. "Time is such an easy thing to spend, but it's not like money. You can't make more."

"Honey, I don't need to be told that. I'm thirty years older than you are."

Ellie laughed. "Luke is supposed to be here in a few

minutes, so if you could leave the door unlocked I'd appreciate it."

"Will do." Maryann headed for the door, then turned back. "When you get done talking to Doc, tell him I wouldn't mind some company for supper. About seven o'clock."

"I'll pass it along." She went over and knocked on Doc's office. "Uncle Don?" she called out, poking her head around the exam room door when he didn't answer.

"Wh— Huh?" Doc sat up, blinking owlishly at her.

Judging from the placement of the chair and the creases in his forehead from the leather top of his old desk, he'd been asleep, just as Maryann had predicted. "I didn't mean to disturb you."

"Not at all, not at all." Doc climbed stiffly to his feet, waving her in. He adjusted his glasses, peering intently at her. "It's nice to see a healthy person for a change, although I don't like to see those bags under your eyes. You look as if you could use a good night's sleep."

"So do you." Ellie came in and sat in the chair opposite his desk. "And I'm afraid I'm going to make that harder for you, at least for the next little while."

"If you're saying you've decided to leave Erskine, Ellie, I'm not surprised. You haven't been happy here."

"I wouldn't have been happy anywhere, Uncle Don, not completely happy. But there have been moments."

"Clary."

"Yes, but that's over."

Doc sank into his chair. "I'm sorry, Ellie, more sorry than you know. I brought you here—"

"It was my decision."

"Nonsense, I manipulated you into it with every weapon at my disposal, including your tragedy. It was wrong of me,

Ellie, and not for that reason alone. You should have stayed in Los Angeles and dealt with what happened."

"Which is exactly why I'm going back."

"What?"

Doc looked toward the door, Ellie turned around, and there stood Luke.

"You're going back to Los Angeles?"

"We're going back," Ellie corrected her brother. "And before you get angry and uncommunicative, sit down and let me tell you everything."

Luke slouched into a chair, avoiding her gaze. "What's there to explain? You broke up with Clary and now you're gonna book. It's what you do whenever things get rough— you leave."

"I know you've had some trouble here, Ellie," Doc said, "but I don't think running away is the solution."

"I'm not running away. Not anymore. I'm going back to L.A. so I can meet with the Brodys. Mathew's family." Panic bubbled inside of her at the thought of it, but she knew it was the right decision. "I don't know if they'll see me but I have to try. I've never spoken to them, and I hope that once I do I'll be able to put this behind me. I'll never forget it—if you don't remember your mistakes you can't learn from them. But I won't have a future as a doctor until I face my past."

She turned to her brother. "I thought you might like to come with me, Luke."

It was Doc who broke the stunned silence. "Are you leaving for good?" he asked, coming around to lean against the front of his desk.

"That's the reason I asked you to meet me here after hours," Ellie said, still talking directly to Luke. "I want you to be part of the decision this time. We can go back for a couple of weeks, or we can go back permanently if you want to take your senior year of high school in Los Angeles."

Luke sat forward. "You're letting me decide?"

"Yes. You don't have to decide now. Wait until we're in L.A. and see how you feel then. If you want to spend the school year in Los Angeles, I'll stay there with you."

"What about Uncle Don?"

"Don't give me another thought," Doc said.

Ellie reached out and squeezed her uncle's hand in thanks. "I knew you'd understand," she said to him, "but if you'll still have me as a partner, I'm planning to return, either two weeks from now or after Luke graduates. I've made friends in this town, and I've begun to build a life here."

"With Clary?" Luke asked.

There it was again, that quick slash of pain at hearing his name. "No, not with Clary."

"Did he dump you?"

Ellie smiled slightly, sadly. "I guess you could say we dumped each other. I didn't think he'd be able to handle what happened to Mathew and my part in it. I should have told him the truth, but he found out on his own, and when he realized I didn't trust him, he was angry."

"And he yelled at you again. This time I'm going to pound him for real."

"I think it might be more constructive if they sit down and talk," Doc said.

"We've done that." Ellie looked away, swallowing to clear the tightness in her throat. "We both said things we can't take back, and we both decided to end it." Okay, that wasn't strictly the truth—she'd decided to end it. But Clary hadn't fought her on it, and that hurt most of all.

"I don't want to meddle, Ellie, but I will say this." Doc

went behind the desk and sat. "Clary is a very decisive man, which makes him apt to rush to judgment, and he was angry and upset. I'm sure he's already regretting whatever it is he said that hurt you so deeply, and you're not a woman who can't forgive."

"I'm a woman with too much going on in my life, Uncle Don. Making the decision to dig myself out of this hole is the easy part. But I learned something from what happened in L.A. It took someone else to make me see it—and, yes, it cost me something precious," she acknowledged. It had cost her the only man she would ever love, but she couldn't think about that now. "I can't turn my feelings off whenever it suits me, but I think I can learn to separate them from the facts. I'm not a miracle worker, and eventually I'm going to lose another patient."

"Yes, and here, in this small community, it will be someone you know."

Her head popped up, her gaze streaking to meet her uncle's. Even though she'd already considered that possibility, she still felt the icy hands of panic close around her heart. The idea that she would lose a friend, or worse, that she wouldn't be able to save one…

"It'll be easier for you to bear," Doc said gently, patting her hand, "if you have somewhere soft to land when your day is done."

He was right, Ellie thought, and all that she had was a soft heart.

THE NEWS RACED through town. Ellie Reed had gone back to L.A., and her brother with her. Work on her house was still going forward, but that only made sense if she was going to try to sell it. Who'd want a half-finished house?

Of course, no one knew the real reason she'd disappeared, which meant there were several rumors, not to mention some pretty wild theories having to do with alien abduction or the Federal witness program. It was Erskine, after all; events didn't always fall into the realm of the normal, but that only made the betting pools more entertaining—and there were several of them regarding Ellie and Luke. And Deputy Sheriff Beeber.

Clary heard the talk, of course, but he didn't subscribe to rumor and innuendo. And he definitely didn't participate in Mike Shasta's illegal gambling operation. But he did believe his eyes and ears. And his heart.

Ellie had left town. That much was clear.

Doc wasn't talking, and Ted Delancey only knew that she and Luke packed up early one morning, didn't say where they were going, just asked him to finish the kitchen.

Clary could have kicked himself. Timing was everything, and he'd blown it twice, first by confronting her before he'd taken time to cool down, and then by backing off. She just needed time, he'd told himself, and she'd accept his apology. It would be kind of hard to deliver it again, though, if he didn't know where to find her.

For one brief, insane moment, he'd considered putting out an APB. Except that was exactly the sort of thing that had gotten him into trouble with Ellie in the first place. She'd hardly thank him for being pulled over by the police and questioned on some bogus matter. Plus, it would get him in hot water over having falsified police records—which, he realized belatedly, should've been his first consideration. But love made you do crazy things, not to mention stupid, thoughtless, selfish ones.

A week after her disappearance found him at her place at twilight, as he'd been every night since she'd gone. No lights were on, and although the weather was fine, with a fresh, cool breeze and a sunset so beautiful it almost made the heart ache, the doors and windows were tightly shut. Even without those clues he'd have known she wasn't there. Ellie was the living, breathing soul of the house, and the soul was missing.

He should've gone back to his cramped apartment and tried to sleep. Instead he made his way around the side of the house toward the back porch. As long as he was here, where they'd been so happy, it was easier to believe things would work out between them.

"I knew you'd show up here sooner or later."

"Sam." Clary stopped where he was and studied his best friend.

Sam was sitting on the porch railing, leaning against a post. Even in the fading light Clary could tell he was pissed off.

"Shouldn't you be home feeding your stock?"

"I had something more important to do." Sam unfolded his tall, lean frame and stalked over to Clary. His fists were balled, but he stopped a couple of feet away.

"If you're going to take a shot at me, Sam, go ahead. I deserve it."

Sam glared at him a couple more minutes, then dropped his hands. "It would make me feel better, that's for sure. But it looks like you're beating yourself up enough already."

Clary would've felt better if Sam had pounded on him. Or maybe not. Maybe he'd just have a sore jaw to go with his sore heart, because he still wouldn't have Ellie. "Do you know where she is, Sam?"

"Do you have any idea how much you hurt her?"

"She got me back. In spades." He shook his head. "She says it's over, Sam."

"And don't think I wouldn't make a play for her if I thought she was interested." Sam shoved his hands in his pockets, kicking at a tuft of weeds. "She's my friend, Clary. So are you—unless you don't do whatever it takes to get her back. It would be bad for my image to hang around with someone that stupid."

"Hopefully my stupid moments are past."

"Yeah, you keep telling yourself that."

"I'd be on my knees now if I knew where to find her," Clary said.

"Maybe Doc Tyler knows."

"Doc flat-out refused to say what he and Ellie talked about her last day at the clinic, and I didn't want to push him." He glanced over at his best friend, surprised at how much it pained him to remember that conversation. "He didn't hit me either, Sam, but he looked like he wanted to."

Sam whistled through his teeth. "Can't remember ever knowing Doc to consider violence."

"Well, I feel like banging my head against a brick wall, so why should anyone else feel different?"

Chapter Seventeen

Erskine felt like home. The morning Ellie got back, she walked the two miles into town and couldn't believe how happy it made her to see the false-fronted buildings, washed with a watercolor dawn, looking as if they'd sprung right out of a Norman Rockwell painting. If she could still feel like she was coming home after the heart-break she'd suffered, then Erskine was where she belonged.

No matter what else happened in her life, she knew that at least there'd be peaceful days spent puttering in her garden and evenings spent sitting on her back porch, watching the apples in her orchard grow and mature. She wished she didn't see herself alone in those moments, but that decision had been made as well, and she was going to have her hands full with being a doctor—a good one.

Just walking into the clinic bumped her stress to an uncomfortable level. She did some deep breathing exercises as she made her way to the tiny office she shared with Doc, and when she heard the clinic door open, she called out, "I could use some tea, Maryann. Something decaffeinated."

She didn't get an answer, and Maryann wasn't at her desk, so she went to the waiting-room door. When she found Clary standing uncertainly in the middle of the waiting room her heart shot up into her throat.

"I saw the lights," he said, taking his hat off and clutching it by the brim. "When did you get back to town?"

No amount of deep breathing was going to calm her this time, Ellie knew. Only sheer, brute willpower would get her through this. "Last night." Her throat eased up as she spoke, but the pain that had tried to strangle her didn't go away; it only moved down into her chest. "I thought I'd come into town and see if Doc needed help today."

His eyes flicked up to meet hers. The blue she'd always thought so warm, now looked pale and washed out. He came over, stopping a couple of feet from her. "Does that mean you're back for good?"

"I was always coming back for good, but I left it up to Luke to decide when."

"You left a decision like that up to a teenager?"

"It's his life, too," she said, and since they weren't talking about their relationship, her upset dropped to a level she could handle. "I made the decision for him last time, and we both know how that worked out. I let him make the choice whether he finished high school in the city or came back here. He chose Erskine, but either way I'd have come back eventually."

"Ellie, I…"

The pain in her chest intensified, radiating out until her whole body seemed to ache with it. "What do you want, Clary?"

"I want to be forgiven."

"You're forgiven." The feel of his hand on her arm, his

fingers warming her cold, cold skin, caused tears to swim in her eyes.

"I wish you meant that, Ellie."

"I do mean it." She sighed, felt some of the tightness finally loosen. He sounded every bit as miserable as she was, and it was foolish for her to punish them both by holding a grudge. "I hurt you, Clary." She turned to face him. "I can understand how it must've felt to know I was keeping secrets. You didn't mean what you said. I know that."

"But?"

"I went back to L.A. to see the Brodys, to give them peace so that when I came back here, I might be able to find some peace of my own. I'm still working with Doc, but the fear's still there, Clary, so if you want to send me packing before I hurt somebody, you'd better do it now. Otherwise, stay out of my way."

In one convulsive reaction, his hands crushed his hat into a shapeless ball. "You still think I'm going to judge you? Do you think I don't live with the same fear every day? Hell, I carry around a gun. There might not be a lot of crime in Erskine, but it only takes once, one time I pull this—" he laid a hand on his holster "—and make the wrong split-second decision, and somebody is hurt, maybe dead. You help people every day. So do I. I think that balances the scales."

"Not for the loved ones who are left behind."

"No, they have to live with it and so do we."

"I know that, Clary. I'm not asking you to help me justify waking up every morning to the chance I'll have to make a life and death choice that day, and that it could be the wrong choice."

"Because you don't think I can handle it."

"I don't think it's fair to put you in that position."

"That's bullshit, Ellie, and you know it. You're still hiding, only this time you're hiding from your own heart. I hurt you and you're afraid to take the chance I'll hurt you again."

"Get out."

"I let you chase me off once because I thought you could use the distance, but I'll be damned if I make that mistake again." He wrapped his hands around her upper arms and hauled her against him, plastering his mouth to hers.

What began in anger exploded into a full-blown kiss before Ellie found the strength to tear herself out of his arms. She pressed trembling fingers to her lips, the one glance she risked at his face enough to convince her he'd taken her response as a sign of hope. At the moment, she couldn't bear to hope; she needed all her strength to make good on the promises she'd given Doc, and herself.

"I shouldn't have done that," Clary said quietly.

"Please don't apologize again." Ellie pulled a stack of charts over and then slammed them back down on the desk. It was that or throw them at him. She'd fallen in love with a high-handed, stubborn, wonderfully infuriating deputy sheriff, not this groveling, hesitant, unsure man who barely looked her in the eye. "We both need to stop dwelling on the past and move on."

A flash of anger crossed his face, and she nearly smiled. "I really do have a lot to do here," she said instead.

"I only have one more thing to say, Ellie." Clary stooped and retrieved his mangled hat, then, as if he'd read her thoughts, looked her straight in the eye. "I love you." And while she was reeling over that revelation, he hit her with the next. "And you love me."

"That's two things."

"And I'm not giving up. That's three." His face folded into the determined lines she recognized so well. "You'll say it to me one day."

"You're awfully sure of yourself."

"I'm sure of you," Clary corrected her. "A woman like you doesn't give a man everything you gave me, Ellie, unless she's in love with him. And a woman whose feelings run as deep as yours doesn't fall out of love because that man hurt her."

"We hurt each other."

"Then I guess we're even."

"What about trust? Love can't exist without trust."

"And I intend to win yours back again, Ellie. No matter how long it takes."

"Clary, I…I'm not sure what to say. Going back to medicine—it's all I can handle right now."

"I'll wait."

"You shouldn't—"

"Say you don't love me, then." He took a step toward her, but he didn't touch her. Neither of them, she knew, could've stood that. "If you can make me believe it, I'll leave now and I won't come back."

The words he'd dared her to say hovered on the tip of her tongue. She met his gaze; if she was going to say something like that, he deserved to have it said to his face. But one look into his eyes, the blue of them bright and warm again, and the words were gone.

"I knew it." Clary jammed his wrinkled, mutilated hat on his head, turned on his heel then back again. His smile took her breath away. He bent and kissed her on the cheek, so sweetly it brought tears to her eyes.

It took the sound of the clinic door shutting to shake her out of her stupor, and then it was too late to do anything more than curse herself. She'd meant it when she told him she needed to focus on practicing medicine, but now that she'd gone and given him hope, there would be no peace, no room for time to work its healing magic.

Clary had as many faults as the next person, but persistence, she thought with a sigh, was the greatest of them.

IN THE DAYS THAT FOLLOWED, Ellie didn't have a lot of time to dwell on Clary's parting comment, or his kiss, for that matter. Her mornings often began at sunrise with a long drive to an outlying ranch or farm after a night spent dealing with some emergency, usually in the opposite direction. Days at the clinic were somewhat easier—shorter definitely—but she still left there so exhausted she wondered how her uncle had managed the practice alone for so long.

But then, people generally did what they had to do. Or what they set their mind to do. She was living proof of that. Doc had shown faith in her, and how did she repay him? She'd skated through her first couple of months on the job, and then she'd taken a vacation. It was about time she did what she'd come to do. Shoulder the bulk of the patient load so her uncle could finally slow down.

The less time she had to second-guess herself the better, she'd decided, and it seemed to be working. She only asked for Doc's collaboration on the most difficult cases, but Ellie also knew she hadn't been truly tested yet.

"Yeesh, that's cold."

"I'm sorry," Ellie quickly removed the bell of the stethoscope from Janey's blossoming tummy and held it between her hands. "I usually warm it. I guess I forgot."

"You looked as if you were a million miles away."

"Just tired."

"I heard about the Wilson kid," Janey said. "Must have been a long night."

"He's going to be fine. Black and blue, and the cast won't come off for six weeks, but he'll be okay."

"Thanks to you and Doc."

"Thanks to Doc, anyway."

"Well, I for one, am grateful you're here," Janey said. "I love Doc as much as the next person, but in these situations, I prefer having a woman—not to mention a friend— around. I mean, who can better understand the worries and apprehension about pregnancy than another woman?"

And who but a woman doctor could imagine the variety of things that could go wrong? Ellie thought, nearly paralyzed at the idea of trying to deliver Janey's baby. "You're going to the hospital when the time comes, right?"

"Are you kidding? Sarah had her baby at home, and half the town was in attendance."

"Obviously that's not for you."

"I've been through this once already. If I thought it would help, I'd be asking for drugs now. And even if I didn't want the modern conveniences, Noah wouldn't give me a choice. As far as he's concerned, the hospital isn't even good enough, but it's all we've got. He's so uptight about this pregnancy he's practically following me around with a feather bed and a three-course meal—carefully balanced between the basic food groups, I might add."

"He loves you."

"He's an idiot." But there was a smile on Janey's face that said he was her idiot, and she'd dare any other woman to do better.

"Well, I agree with him," Ellie said. "It's important for you to get plenty of rest and eat the right things. And the hospital goes without saying."

"What's wrong?"

"Nothing. You're as healthy as a…" The way Janey's eyes narrowed warned Ellie not to finish that statement.

"So, if I'm not the problem, then what is?"

Ellie drew in a breath and blew it out slowly as she considered the wisdom of answering that question. But in the end, she concluded that Janey deserved the whole truth before she chose who she wanted to take care of her and her baby. "I think there's something you should know before you decide if you want me to deliver your baby."

"Tell me," Janey said immediately.

Ellie helped her sit up on the edge of the table, then took a seat on the little exam stool. It wasn't nearly as difficult to tell her the story of Matthew Brody as it had been to tell Clary, but it still hurt. Seeing Janey's eyes fill with sympathetic tears helped.

"You're probably the last person who wants to hear this, but I keep seeing that boy's face. His parents were wonderful, completely supportive, but I can't seem to put it completely behind me," Ellie finished, miserable over it, but relieved to have it said out loud.

Janey had listened quietly to the story, and even when it was over she didn't say anything right away. Instead of making Ellie nervous, the silence told her that Janey was really digesting what she'd heard and searching inside herself to see how she felt about it.

"It seems to me," Janey said at last, "that someone who's been what you've been through, Ellie, would take pains to be thorough and careful."

Her response, coming from a place of deliberation, meant so much more to Ellie than an instant declaration of support would have. "You'll be in the hospital when your time comes, Janey, and you know Doc will never forgive you if he doesn't get to be there for the big day."

"I'd like you to be there, Ellie. I trust you. So does Doc."

"You're being supportive—and Doc felt sorry for me."

"Doc wouldn't entrust his patients to you out of pity. You know that."

"What if I let him down?"

"I wish I could help, but I've never been very good at coming up with the right words. What do you think your parents would have said?"

"My father used to say nothing worth having came without a fight." Ellie laughed softly, her heart suddenly lighter. "He wasn't afraid of anything, and my mother was right there by his side every step of the way. Thanks for reminding me."

"You're welcome, and since I'm on a roll, what's the deal with you and Clary?"

Ellie rose to her feet and slipped her stethoscope around her neck, then set about putting the room back to rights for the next clinic day. "There is no deal."

"Try that on someone who hasn't just seen every emotion under the sun cross your face—and don't think turning your back on me will make a difference."

"Honestly, Janey, I don't have time for romance right now."

"And you're both miserable. Don't deny it, Ellie. Maybe no one else in this town believes you two were dating, but I know Clary. And I'd like to think I'm beginning to know you."

Ellie shrugged, methodically shredding the wad of

cotton balls she was supposed to be stuffing into the glass jar. "We had a little fling, then we had a big argument. End of story."

Janey snorted rudely. "Look, I'm not asking you what happened, although I'll admit I'm dying to know. Noah would say it's none of my business, but I don't let that stop me any more than anyone else in this town does."

"If you want to help, Janey, you'll stay out of it. I can't tell you right now what happened. Maybe someday, but it's too soon."

"I wish I could say I didn't understand what you mean," Janey said. "There was a time when Noah and I…" She broke off with a watery laugh. "I can't even talk about it now, and everything turned out wonderfully for us.

"I guess what I'm trying to say is don't give up. When your father said the best things in life don't come easy? That goes for love, too. The deeper the love, the more it's worth fighting for. Sometimes it feels as if it's helpless, but if you have a love like that in your life, everything else is bearable."

Ellie smiled, giving in to the impulse to hug Janey, as unprofessional as it might be. As she pulled back the self-satisfied smile in the other woman's eyes made her suspicious. "And what did you tell Clary?"

Janey smiled sheepishly. "Pretty much the same thing, only the sentences were a lot shorter and I threw in a few cuss words to make sure I had his complete attention. He is a man, after all," she added with a laugh.

"Clary's never had a problem with his attention span."

"True, but if there's not food, sports or sex involved, men tend to need some encouragement—and let me point out that this is the last time I intend to tell him what to do.

I have my hands full with the one I married. From now on, Clary is your problem."

"I doubt that, Janey. I've barely seen him for two weeks."

"Oh, I have a feeling that's about to change."

Chapter Eighteen

How, Clary wondered, was he supposed to court a woman who worked seven days a week, practically twenty-four hours a day?

He managed to catch her at the diner a couple of times, once for breakfast, and once for lunch. He joined her despite the fact that each time she was poring over medical texts or magazines and clearly didn't want to be disturbed. By the time those meals were over, he'd succeeded in turning her frowns into smiles, if guarded ones. Clary understood completely. She was coming back to him, but neither of them could really open up under the scrutiny of the townspeople. He needed to have her to himself, someplace away from curious eyes.

Sunday was the only day Ellie had off, and even then she usually got called out to some distant ranch or farm. Clary went to her house early in the morning; he didn't figure she'd be awake yet, but he found her perched on a ladder, her bare arms and clothing smudged with the same cream-colored paint she was slapping on the trim of the rear-porch roof.

She'd pulled her hair back from her face and braided it. He couldn't see more than the curve of her cheek, the line of her neck, but that braid made her look young and carefree as it swung with each movement. Or maybe it was the outfit any teenage girl might have worn—baggy, low-slung jeans and a tank top that bared her belly every time she reached up.

For a moment Clary thought it was his blood singing in his ears, then he separated the steady drum of his pulse from the sweet sound of her voice. She was humming. Off-key. She painted to the music, her wrist flicking back and forth like a conductor's baton.

She looked so slight and delicate, but there was such strength in her. After everything she'd been through in her life, that she could get up every morning and face each day amazed him, let alone that she could do it with such optimism and energy.

Love caught him by the throat, swift enough to squeeze the air from his lungs. If he'd taken the time to think about what he was doing, he would never have walked over to the ladder, wrapped his hands around her waist and lifted her down. She gave a shriek, and the paintbrush went flying into the shrubbery so she could brace her hands on his shoulders, her body sliding inch by inch down his.

"What—"

He silenced her with his mouth, didn't merely kiss her, *possessed* her. She was his; the time had come to stop talking about it and show her. So he held her tight and when she melted into him, when he felt her surrender, he swept her up into his arms and carried her into the house.

"Clary, I…"

"Don't."

It wasn't the word that made her mute, it was the way he ground it out, as though he walked a thin line between control and violence and one word, the wrong word, could push him too far. And yet she knew if she said no, he'd stop instantly. That unquestioning trust bloomed inside her with all the warmth and light of the sunrise after a long, cold night. Then he set her on her feet beside her bed and looked her over from head to toe, blue eyes shimmering like flame in the dimness of her bedroom.

There was only the whisper of cloth, the slight breeze billowing the curtains and wafting across her skin as he undressed her, then himself, never taking his eyes from hers. The thrill of danger moved through her, and she let out a slight gasp when he reached for her, but it wasn't fear. It was excitement that rose to a fever pitch as he picked her up again and placed her on the bed, following her down so that the whole glorious length of him covered her.

She probably would've begged him to hurry, if she'd been able to force any words past the need that tightened her throat. It wouldn't have been necessary. Clary had always been gentle, even when she could tell he wanted her desperately. This time there were no soft words, no easing her into ecstasy before he joined their bodies and sought his own pleasure.

He took her; that was the only way to describe it. He pushed her ruthlessly to the edge, then drove into her just as her climax burst through her and she cried out at the intensity of the pleasure.

When she could think again, see again, he was lying on his side next to her, an elbow propping up his head so he could look into her face. The blue eyes she loved so much wouldn't meet hers, and the expression on his face made her heart sink. "If you apologize, I'll…" She couldn't think of anything suitably nasty so she elbowed him in the ribs.

He caught her before she could slip off the bed. "I didn't hurt you?"

"Hurt me?" She flopped back down, but he looked so uncertain the laughter died in her throat. "I probably shouldn't admit this, but every woman wants to be over-powered now and again. As long as she knows there's no real danger." She reached up to brush the sun-bleached hair back from his forehead. "I knew you wouldn't hurt me, Clary."

"That's trust."

Ellie sighed. "That's trust."

His smile made her heart turn over in her chest.

"You're a sneaky, persistent man, Deputy Sheriff. There doesn't seem to be a defense you can't worm your way around."

He gathered her into his arms and held her, just held her. She nestled in and closed her eyes. She would've been content to stay that way forever, but the world, in the form of a cell phone, intruded.

They both jerked upright and dove for their clothing before Ellie recognized the somber tones of Beethoven—*da-da-da-dummmm*—and realized it wasn't hers.

"That was supposed to be a joke," Clary mumbled. He answered it, saying nothing more than a couple of uh-huhs before hanging up again. "Old man Winston's cows are in the road again."

Ellie got up, pulling her own clothing on as he dressed, clipping her cell phone in its little holster onto her belt loop.

"That's handy," Clary said.

"You have your weapon, I have mine." She tucked the phone away, self-consciously rubbing at some of the paint streaking her arms. "Doc's way out in the country, so I'm on call. There always seems to be some kind of emergency on Sunday."

She kept her back to him, but when his hands settled on her shoulders it was too much for her battered emotions to bear.

She turned and wrapped her arms around his waist, burying her face in his shirt and taking a deep, deep breath of the crisp scent of him. "Let old man Winston deal with his own cows. Stay here with me."

"It's my job. I know you hate it when I say that, but it's the truth."

"Maybe it's time you got Mr. Winston to fix his fence so he doesn't have to call you every other day."

He gave her a kiss that was so sweet and gentle it brought tears to her eyes. "You tell me what makes you happy, Ellie, and I'll do it."

The resignation on his face, coupled with a lost-little-boy look of hope made her laugh softly. "I'm not foolish enough to try to change you and think you'll still be the man I fell in love with."

"Love?" He crushed her to him, lifted her clear off her feet and peppered her face and throat with kisses, murmuring those same three words over and over before spinning her in a circle then setting her on her feet. He tucked his arm around her waist and pulled her firmly against his side. "I thought you were going to keep me waiting forever," he said.

"That kind of…slipped out." And left her fighting for breath. She pulled away and walked through the house and out the back door.

He stopped her at the edge of the orchard, whirling her around. "You're not shutting me out this time."

She covered her face with her hands, then fisted them in her hair like he'd seen her do whenever she got frustrated. "I don't want to need you like this, Clary."

"But you do, and I'm the happiest, most grateful man on earth because of it." But he could see she was still troubled. "I don't have to go—"

"Yes, you do."

"I could call Sam."

"Sam's busy. You'd hate to take him away from his work."

"I think I could make that sacrifice for you," he said dryly.

"Maybe today, but in time you'd resent me for it."

He smiled, one eyebrow raised. "In time? Does that mean you see this relationship going somewhere...interesting?"

"I have a feeling anything that involves you will be interesting, whether I want it to be or not."

"I hope so." He kissed her on the tip of her nose. "And when I return, we're going to discuss this relationship and get a few things straight."

Her brow furrowed. "Clary—"

"Don't analyze it to death, Dr. Reed. All you can do is take it as it comes."

Ellie shaded her eyes to watch him walk away, frowning as, halfway to the house he turned and came back to her, slowly took his hat off and leaned down to place a soft, lingering kiss on her lips. "I love you," he said, his smile more dazzling than the sun in the sky. He stared at her intently, chuckling when she began to fidget self-consciously. "I intend to say that to you for a long time to come." His hand came up to cup her cheek, his thumb rubbing along the line of her jaw. He dropped his hat on his head at rakish angle and sauntered away, saying, "I'll see you later," over his shoulder.

"I'm going to hold you to that, Deputy Sheriff," she called after him, laughing when he saluted her with two fingers to the brim of his hat.

As he drove away, she began to search the shrubbery for her paintbrush, wondering how in the world she was going to paint when it felt as if she was floating—

Tires squealed and a horrendous crash tore through the peaceful Sunday quiet. And she knew. She just knew.

ELLIE DIDN'T REMEMBER racing into her house to grab her keys and medical bag from the kitchen. She didn't remember jumping into her car or running her own mailbox down as she backed out of her driveway. Clary was hurt, the certainty of it sat on her chest like a lead weight, but even half prepared for it, the extent of the accident left her almost numb with disbelief.

Her car slewed to an uneven stop at the side of the road, and for a precious moment, she could only stare at Clary's SUV, pretzeled around the front of a semi in the middle of the very intersection he'd warned her about so often. The passenger side had taken the main force of the impact; she was thankful for that until she came around and looked in through the shattered driver's window.

Smoke from the air bag filled the inside of the Blazer. Ellie wrenched at the door, kicking and screaming when it wouldn't open. She would have climbed in through the window if someone hadn't pulled her down and set her aside. She fought to return to Clary, but somewhere in the panic she understood the other person was helping when a crowbar was slipped in the crack between the door and the frame of the vehicle. Almost before the two separated with the shriek of metal on metal, she was through the opening.

She checked Clary over with shaking hands, feeling for broken bones and prodding at his belly. Though he was unconscious, she saw no reaction that would've led her to believe there was any internal damage. With the exception of a few cuts and the fact that he'd almost certainly have some spectacular bruising, he seemed to have come through it pretty well unharmed.

As if to prove it, his eyes fluttered open, and he gave her a slight, trembling smile. He opened his mouth. Nothing came out but a wheezing hiss of air. Frowning, he wrapped his hand around Ellie's and squeezed so hard she felt her bones grind together. He tried to speak again and couldn't.

Ellie's heart stopped beating.

"Here, miss, let's get him out of there."

She looked over and saw a big, burly man standing beside the open door, tears in his eyes.

"I was driving the truck," he said, then gently but firmly helped her out of the SUV. "We have to get him to the nearest hospital."

"The nearest hospital is an hour away, but I'm a doctor," she said, cradling Clary's head as the man pulled him from the Blazer and laid him carefully on the warm concrete surface of the road. "There's a black bag in the front seat of my car—"

He was gone before she could finish the sentence. Ellie focused on Clary again, one hand tearing her phone out of its pouch and speed-dialing Doc Tyler by feel, the other ripping open his shirt and lifting the T-shirt beneath to examine his chest again. "No broken ribs," she muttered, almost screaming in frustration when a recording came on to say her call couldn't be completed. Her bag appeared at her side, and she ripped it open, pulling out her stethoscope.

"Stay with me, Clary," she said, pleased to see his eyelids flicker as if he'd heard her. She listened to his heart, going cold when she noticed his heartbeat was slow and growing fainter. His lungs were quiet. Too quiet and barely moving. "Pneumothorax?"

"What?"

She glanced over, into the worried, unshaven face of the truck driver. "He's not getting enough air. Could be a collapsed lung... I'm not sure."

"You said you were a doctor—"

"Trying to treat a man in the middle of the road with no way to run tests or take X-rays," she lashed out. She blinked her eyes, then realized it was her hand shaking, not tears that made it hard to focus on the phone. "C'mon, Doc, be there." The call connected this time but she caught only a syllable here and there before the connection failed.

She tossed the useless phone aside and felt Clary's pulse again then tried mouth-to-mouth, barely discerning the rise and fall of his chest. "What do I do?" She grabbed the trucker's arm and shook him. "Doc's in the middle of nowhere and I can't reach him. I don't know what to do."

She got to her feet and paced, fists pounding at her temples in an attempt to think through the fear gripping her.

"Miss! Doctor! I don't think he's breathing anymore."

Ellie raced back to Clary and fell on her knees beside him, the pain of rocks biting into her skin slicing through the hysteria. He was still breathing. His breaths were shallow and wheezy, but she hadn't lost him. And she didn't intend to. Even if she made the wrong diagnosis, she told herself, at least she'd be doing something instead of standing back and letting him die. "If he had a collapsed lung, his chest wouldn't have risen at all when I did mouth-to-mouth," she said, feeling stronger and a bit more calm.

"There has to be some other reason he can't breathe." She checked his ribs again, then his sternum, clamping down on the nerves that made her want to race through the examination. She had to go slowly and be thorough. Clary's life depended on it.

"Nothing broken," she concluded as she checked his collarbones and found them sound, "so his lungs can't be punctured. It has to be his trachea." Sure enough a bruise was blossoming on his throat. "Which is why he couldn't speak." If she hadn't lost herself to panic she would've realized that sooner. She prayed it wasn't too late. Whatever the damage, it would only get worse as the tissues in his throat swelled further from the injury until he wouldn't be able to breathe at all.

Fear caught her by the heart again, constricting her chest so she had to fight to think past it. One look into Clary's still face had her taking hold with both hands. She laid her cheek against his and said, "I love you, Clary, hang in there."

She straightened in time to see his eyes open, warm and blue as they gazed into hers with such love and faith it felt like a soothing breeze had come up and blown the fear right out of her. Purpose replaced it, along with a solid core of determination. She nodded once and knew he understood her. He wasn't going anywhere as long as she was around.

Ellie picked up her phone and dialed Sam Tucker's number, breathing a silent prayer of thanks when she heard Sam's voice loud and clear. "Don't ask questions, Sam," she said. "Just bring your truck to the intersection between my house and town. Now."

She took a clean, white towel out of her bag, laying out the things she would need, clipping the ends off a plastic syringe. She even smiled grimly when she glanced up and saw the truck driver's face go pale and clammy.

"You look like you haven't slept in a while. If you don't want more on your conscience than you already have, you'd better pull yourself together and help me."

Ellie didn't wait for his agreement, simply ordered him to pull on a pair of rubber gloves as she did. She let her breath out in a long, slow, steadying exhale, and looked into Clary's face one last time. His lips were turning blue. He wasn't breathing, and his pulse, when she set her fingers on his wrist, was nonexistent, banishing the last dregs of uncertainty.

Either she did something or Clary died. It was that simple.

"Okay, here goes." She picked up the disinfectant and poured it over Clary's neck, swabbing away the excess that puddled in the hollow of his throat with sterile gauze. She took up the scalpel in her left hand, laid the tips of her fingers on his throat and felt her way down the rings of cartilage that made up the larynx, talking herself through the process the whole time. At the first cut, she heard a muffled thump and saw that the truck driver had passed out. No matter; she'd grow a third hand if she needed it.

By the time it came to that, Sam was pulling up in a slide of gravel and a shower of dust that thankfully blew in the other direction. Ellie finished the incision, through the skin and the tougher tracheal tissue beneath and slipped the short length of syringe through the opening. The tissue closed around it, exactly as it was supposed to.

"Jesus." Sam came up beside her, looking from the mangled wreckage of Clary's SUV to his still face and bloody neck. "What happened?"

She ignored the question, bending to put her mouth around the end of the syringe and blow with every ounce of strength she possessed. His chest rose, fell, and didn't rise again. "He's not breathing on his own and I can't get a pulse. Damn it, Clary!" She threaded her fingers together, but before she could start CPR, she was shoved gently aside.

"Let me," Luke said. When she hesitated he added, "You made me take first aid, remember?"

And he'd complained the entire time, Ellie recalled, but she knew Luke. He might have resented going, but he'd taken the class seriously.

She nodded, settling on her knees beside Clary again, prepared to blow into the plastic syringe in between Luke's compressions. "Go to my house and get some blankets, Sam."

"Clary always carries some in the back of the SUV for emergencies. I'll lay them out in the back of my truck."

She nodded as she bent to give Clary another breath of much-needed air, paused while Luke did another round of compressions, then blew again. Clary's chest rose and fell, and the fingers she'd placed on his carotid pulse felt a faint kick. More compressions, another breath of air and that fluttering strengthened. She felt the first slight spontaneous movement of air through Clary's makeshift airway and sat back on her heels, looking up into Sam's worried face.

"We need to get him to the hospital. Now."

Chapter Nineteen

Clary opened his eyes, blinked them a couple of times and shut them against the unfamiliar glare of light over his head. He started to drift back to sleep, but something nagged at him, several things, actually, like the bare white walls and the odd noises that floated to him. His apartment was paneled with warm golden pine and this time of year he'd wake to the sounds of summer through his open window. Birds chirping or maybe a light rain eased him into each day. Or Ellie did.

But Ellie wasn't there; he wasn't sure of much, but Clary would've known if she was in the same room with him. They'd made up, hadn't they? He fought to remember, but only snatches came back to him, Ellie perched on a ladder humming and painting, Ellie beneath him as they made love, Ellie standing between the house and the orchard, watching him walk away. And then her face, stained with tears, her voice, pleading one minute, bawling him out the next.

And pain.

He shied away from that last recollection and the ones that followed it, strange faces staring down at him, voices

strained and expressions severe. He wanted to think only
of Ellie, to put those bits of memory into some kind of realistic timeline so he could rest in the knowledge that they
were together again, that hearing her say "I love you"
wasn't just a figment of his imagination. Even his cop's
mind couldn't manage to make sense of it before exhaustion dragged him from consciousness.

The next time he woke the light was natural, although
the reflection of it off the bare white walls had him squint-
ing. The room wasn't entirely unfamiliar—like something
he'd seen in a dream, or—

The accident came roaring back as if it was just happening. Clary threw a hand up to shield his face, such pain
searing through him that all he could do was collapse
against the mattress while each breath he drew burned like
fire in his throat.

"Clary!"

Soft, cool hands stroked his hair back from his brow,
and a warm, damp cloth that smelled faintly of lemon
cleansed the sweat from his face.

He opened his eyes, drank in the sight of Ellie, dark eyes
filled with concern.

"What—" It came out somewhere between a whisper
and a croak, and hurt like hell.

She moved around the bed to retrieve the plastic
hospital cup from the table, and when she held the straw
to his mouth, he studied her face. He took a long sip,
noting the shadows under her eyes and the lines of strain
around her mouth. Her dusky skin was pale with fatigue
and her hair looked dull, the long braid ragged and
unkempt. She wore loose green hospital scrubs, but there
were still traces of paint on her arms.

"Take another sip," she said, her voice low and soothing. "I know it hurts, but your throat needs the moisture."

He did as she asked, and although it hurt to swallow, the water sliding down his throat was blessedly cool. He opened his mouth, but Ellie cut him off before he got out the first syllable.

"Don't try to talk, Clary. You had an accident, and your throat was badly damaged. A tracheotomy had to be done so you could breathe, but you're in the hospital now. The surgeons have repaired the damage to your trachea and closed the incision, but you're going to be sore for a while."

"Hurts," he whispered, his entire body convulsing at the agony of saying that one word.

"Shh."

He felt her weight settle on the edge of the bed. She stroked his forehead, and whispered over his closed eyes. "Sleep is the best thing for you right now."

Clary felt himself floating away under the soothing comfort of those cool, gentle hands, but the sensation of her getting up jolted him awake. "Ellie—"

She clasped her hand around one of his and bent over him. "I love you."

He could only mouth the words back to her, but he fell asleep with them on his lips.

MOST OF A WEEK PASSED, five days, Clary counted, making seven in all since the accident. Sam and Luke had been there almost every day, and Janey and Noah had come twice. Half the town had made an appearance, as evidenced by the assortment of flowers, plants and baked goods adorning every flat surface in the room. Doc had been in each morning, along with the surgeon who'd operated on him, and there seemed to be nurses everywhere. What was missing was Ellie.

She came every day, but it was usually late at night or early in the morning. Clary was still sleeping a lot, and no matter how much rest he got during the day, he was so tired by nightfall he could barely keep his eyes open. But he saw enough of her to know she was struggling, despite the bright smile she always greeted him with. He needed to talk to her, to find out what was going on in that mind of hers. Another day passed before he figured out a way to do it, but then, he wasn't at his best at present.

In fact, coming up with the plan was a lot easier than carrying it out. His head swam when he got out of bed, and every time he moved, something hurt, but he managed to dress himself by the time Sam and Luke arrived for their daily visit. And since Clary figured his intentions were obvious, he didn't waste energy talking, simply walked out of his room and past the nurses' station.

By the time he'd shuffled to the elevator at the end of the hallway, he had a regular parade stretched out behind him. Sam and Luke, of course, a couple of ambulatory patients and at least two nurses, both of whom were chattering nonstop about rules and trying to shepherd him back to his room. If Sam and Luke hadn't taken up positions on either side of him when they got to the elevator, no doubt the ladies in white would've been successful because, frankly, Clary couldn't have fended off a hummingbird in his condition.

"You sure about this?" Sam muttered.

"Ellie's avoiding me," Clary rasped.

Sam sighed. "I'm going to catch hell, y'know."

"Me, too," Luke put in.

"If she has any mad left over when she's through with me."

"You've got a point," Sam said to Clary. "Don't leave without me." He flipped the keys to Luke, punched the elevator call button, and pasted a killer grin on his face. "Ladies," he said, winding an arm around each nurse's waist, "why don't we talk about this?" In seconds he had them giggling and blushing—back at the nurses' station

"Do you think he could teach me that on the drive home?" Clary asked Luke.

"Not even if home was a couple thousand miles away," Luke replied. When Clary scowled at him, he added hastily, "It wouldn't work on Ellie, anyway."

No, charm definitely wouldn't work on Ellie, Clary thought morosely. Going back to his hospital room wouldn't do the trick, either, so he stepped into the elevator when it came, knowing he had two hours to figure out what would. Unfortunately, he dozed most of the ride back to Erskine, and when the cessation of movement jolted him awake he discovered that half the town was gathered in front of the clinic. Waiting for him, apparently.

He sent Sam a bleary-eyed glare.

"Wasn't me or Luke," Sam said. "Doc probably called to warn Ellie you were on your way."

Clary sighed, wondering why he'd expected any less. "I don't see Ellie, but it looks as if the rest of the town turned out."

Luke had already jumped out of the back of the truck and was opening the door. Several of the men in town scrambled forward to assist Clary. They spent a great deal of time and went to a great deal of trouble to prop him up against the front bumper, and then they started to talk, all at once sometimes. Aside from hearing Ellie's voice, it was the most wonderful noise in the world to Clary. Because he was home.

"We've been walking the town," Lem Darby said, "me, Mike Shasta, Sam and some of the other men, morning and night, just like you always do, Clary. Sam is acting deputy, but he's so busy we're all taking turns being on call, in case something happens."

"Of course, Lem, being newly married, isn't taking the night shift very much," Owen Keller shouted out, to the delight of the crowd.

"You got married this week, Lem? Congratulations."

Lem shook the hand Clary held out. "We didn't want to wait," he said, flushing from the neck of his postal shirt to the edge of his receding hairline, "but Edie wants to have a party, right and proper, in a couple of weeks when you're well enough to come and dance with Dr. Ellie."

"If she'll have him," Sam contributed.

"She will," Maisie Cunningham shouted over the laughter. "Got me a five-dollar bill that says so."

"And I say she won't," Ted Delancey called out.

"Well, if you're starting a pool, count me in," Clary said.

This statement was followed by absolute and utter silence, and then someone from the back of the crowd said tentatively, "That wouldn't be fair, Clary, you having the inside track and all."

"Do you think I'm going to let anybody win a pool about my life but me?"

Clary's questions resulted in another round of speech-lessness, so that when Janey pushed open the clinic door and said, "Uh-oh," it practically echoed off the buildings lining the street.

The silent citizens of Erskine swiveled to look at her.

"The only time I've seen this town so quiet is in memoriam,

on the major patriotic holidays," she said. "I'd be concerned, Clary, if I didn't see you standing there with my own eyes." She came over to hug him. "It's good to see you."

"Same goes," Clary said, hugging her back. "I thought Doc was still at the hospital."

"He is. I had an appointment with Ellie. She's delivering my baby."

"Really? That's great, Janey."

But he must've appeared troubled or shocked or something, because Janey moved closer, so the rest of the town wouldn't hear her say, "Ellie told me everything."

"And you trust her."

It wasn't a question, but Janey answered it, anyway. "She took what happened so much to heart, Clary, and she's dedicated to making sure it doesn't happen again, so how could I not trust her? And even if I'd had my doubts before, they'd be put to rest now. She's turned a corner. Your accident—"

The crowd had been winding up again, talking and laughing, but the noise cut off suddenly once more. Because Ellie had stepped through the clinic door. An aisle opened magically between where she stood and where Clary leaned against Sam's pickup, all his friends getting out of their way. Including Janey.

Clary exchanged a look with Luke, who held up his hands and backed off. No help there.

"Sam," Ellie said into the silence, "take the deputy sheriff to his apartment. Or better yet, take him to my house where I can keep an eye on him."

Hoots and hollers sounded out, and someone yelled

good-naturedly, "What kind of example is that to set for the youngsters?"

"We're getting married as soon as I can get her to say yes," Clary shot back.

Ellie, not even cracking a smile, tucked her hands in the pockets of her lab coat. "I don't think I want to marry someone pigheaded and idiotic enough to check himself out of the hospital against the advice of his doctors."

"I'm not going anywhere without you," Clary said. "How's that for pigheaded?"

"I'll be there later. I have patients to see."

Maryann, who'd been poking her head out the clinic door, said, "The last two appointments were just routine checkups, Dr. Ellie, and they were only too happy to reschedule."

The look in Clary's eyes said he would outlast her no matter what it cost him. The tightness around his jaw told Ellie it would cost him a lot—and she wasn't prepared to watch him pay that price so she could prove she was more stubborn.

She returned to the clinic, exchanged her lab coat for her purse, and went back out again, climbing into Sam's pickup. Luke opted to stay in town for a while. Big surprise. If he'd been trying to afford them privacy he could've spared himself the trouble. Clary was asleep by the time they made the two-mile drive to her house. He woke up long enough to stumble up the stairs and peel off his clothes before he collapsed into bed and drifted off.

Ellie sat in a chair across the room and watched him sleep. Even when he began to stir a couple of hours later, she didn't leave. She did, however, cover up the pain and anxiety of seeing him so pale and weak. She'd let him have his way in the street so he didn't fall over and reinjure himself. He was flat on his back now; no way was she letting him off the hook again.

"You should've stayed in the hospital," she said when he awoke.

He looked at her and held out a hand that shook slightly. So much emotion filled her heart and lodged in her throat that there was no room for anger.

She came over and took his hand, sitting next to him on the bed. "You're not nearly well enough to be home yet."

"I figured it was the only way to get you to talk to me."

Before the accident his voice had been deep and smooth, now it held a rough edge that would likely always be there, a permanent reminder that he'd almost died.

He had died, and she nearly hadn't brought him back.

"Why are you staying away?" he asked.

Ellie looked down, watching his thumb rub over the back of her hand. "Doc has been splitting his time between here and the clinic, so I've been handling the rest of the territory—and it's a big territory. Some people are even asking for me in particular." Her smile turned a bit sad. "I guess I've earned a new reputation since your accident."

"Sam told me what you did. Operating on me right there in the street, and then bullying him into driving while you rode in the back with me all the way to the hospital. It must have been a hell of a ride, Ellie."

Hellish was more like it. They'd gotten Clary onto the blankets Sam had laid out in the bed of his pickup, since it was the only way they had to transport him. Then Sam wrung every ounce of horsepower out of the old thing while Luke and the truck driver kept Clary from rolling around. She'd been less adept at keeping herself from getting banged up, but getting Clary to the hospital alive had been the only thing that mattered, and every bruise, every ache and pain had been worth it. "Even with Sam taking curves on two wheels and breaking every speed limit on the way, it felt like it took us forever to get here."

"I'll have to give him a ticket."

Ellie laughed, sniffing back her tears. "He's acting deputy sheriff until you get back on your feet, so that might be kind of hard. Besides which, he saved your life—"

"You saved my life."

She made a wordless sound of denial.

"That's what Doc told me. And Sam said he got there just as you finished…working on me, and I had no pulse."

"Only for a few seconds."

Clary gave a scratchy laugh. "That's dead in my book."

"It shouldn't have come to that." It took all her strength to look in him in the face. "It wouldn't have, if I hadn't hesitated."

"Ellie—"

"That's what happened out there, Clary. You were lying in the middle of the road, barely breathing, and I couldn't decide what to do. I tried to call Doc, but I couldn't get hold of him."

"You were there," he said simply. "Doc told me you did as good a job of field surgery as any he's ever seen. I'll barely have a scar."

But he would have one, Ellie thought, and it would always remind her that he had died in her arms.

He took her chin in his hand, tilting her face up until she met his eyes. "I can only imagine how I would've felt if it had been you lying there, and me knowing what could happen if I made the wrong decision. You didn't, Ellie. You were afraid, but you did what you had to do to save my life."

"I know." She smiled at the surprise on his face. "It was a heck of a way to finish teaching me that lesson. You pushed me into dealing with my past, and then forced me to face my fear of making a mistake. It's still there—fear isn't something that goes away. It's something you have to work through and live through, and maybe each time you do it gets a little easier, but it never completely goes away. You just have to live your life as it comes."

He smiled suddenly, that smile that always stole her breath. "I can tell you what's coming. We're going to get married and live in your house. My apartment's way too small for four kids."

She lifted a brow. "Four?"

"Boy, girl, boy, girl. In that order."

"Four pregnancies and a very demanding full-time job," she mused. "Not to mention midnight feedings, potty training. We're going to be busy for the next few years."

"I guess it's a good thing my job is so peaceful."

"But it's awfully demanding, Clary, and so is mine. If we get married, there will be days we don't spend five minutes together."

"*When* we're married we'll have to make sure there are other days we shut off the phones and ignore the rest of the world."

Ellie met his eyes, and for once he couldn't tell what she was thinking or feeling.

"I love you, Ellie," he said, toying with her fingers in his sudden nervousness.

Those quiet words, the exact ones she'd needed to hear,

drained every emotion from her but one. Love swelled in her so fast and overwhelming she felt as if it shone from her.

"We're both hardheaded and we both have demanding careers," Clary said when she didn't respond, "but if I thought my job would get in the way of us building a life together, I'd quit in a heartbeat.

"Besides, everyone in town has been bugging me to take time off. I figure I have about a year of vacation added up by now, and I intend to start by taking a honeymoon."

Ellie made a sound, part exasperation, part amusement.

"Will you marry me?" Clary asked so fast he stumbled over the words.

"Finally!" But she was smiling so wide her face hurt. "We'll have to do it soon if you want to take that honeymoon."

When he gave her a questioning look, she shrugged. "Doc says he's retiring in a year. I think I can convince him to take some clinic hours, but I'll be handling most of the practice alone." At least until the scholarship program she had in mind got off the ground. It hadn't taken her more than a couple of grueling weeks to come up with the idea. She had no intention of working constantly for the rest of her life like her uncle, and she had no problem helping some underprivileged, deserving student get through medical school, as long as that person reciprocated with a few years of slave labor. "I'm going to be very busy, especially if you intend to start on those four children right away."

Clary gathered her into his arms and Ellie lifted her feet so she could lie on her side next to him.

"Is that a yes?" he asked.

She turned her head up and kissed him lightly on the lips. "Would you settle for any other answer?"

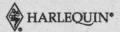
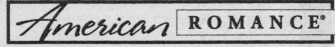

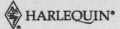

HARLEQUIN®

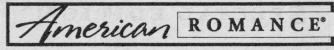

American ROMANCE®

**IS DELIGHTED TO BRING YOU FOUR NEW
BOOKS IN A MINISERIES BY POPULAR AUTHOR**

Jacqueline Diamond

Downhome Doctors

**First-rate doctors
in a town of second chances**

A FAMILY AT LAST
On sale April 2006

Karen Lowell and Chris McRay fell in love in high
school, then everything fell apart their senior year
when Chris had to testify against Karen's brother—
his best friend—in a slaying. The fallout for everyone
concerned was deadly. Now Chris, a pediatrician, is
back in Downhome, and asking Karen for her help....

Also look for:
THE POLICE CHIEF'S LADY
On sale December 2005

NINE-MONTH SURPRISE
On sale February 2006

DAD BY DEFAULT
On sale June 2006

Available wherever Harlequin books are sold.

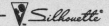
♦ Silhouette®

SPECIAL EDITION™

DON'T MISS THE FIRST BOOK IN
PATRICIA McLINN's
EXCITING NEW SERIES
Seasons in a Small Town

WHAT ARE FRIENDS FOR?
April 2006

When tech mogul Zeke Zeekowsky
returned for his hometown's Lilac Festival,
the former outsider expected a hero's
welcome. Instead, his high school fling,
policewoman Darcie Barrett, mistook him
for a wanted man and handcuffed him!
But the software king and the small-town
girl were quick to make up....

▼ Silhouette®

SPECIAL EDITION™

PRESENTING A NEW MINISERIES BY

RaeANNE THAYNE:

The Cowboys of Cold Creek

BEGINNING WITH

LIGHT THE STARS

April 2006

Widowed rancher Wade Dalton relied
on his mother's help to raise three small
children—until she eloped with "life coach"
Caroline Montgomery's grifter father! Feeling
guilty, Caroline put her Light the Stars
coaching business on hold to help the angry
cowboy...and soon lit a fire in his heart.

DON'T MISS THESE ADDITIONAL BOOKS IN THE SERIES:

DANCING IN THE MOONLIGHT, May 2006
DALTON'S UNDOING, June 2006

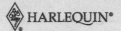

HARLEQUIN®

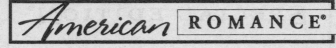

American ROMANCE®

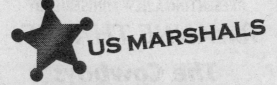

US MARSHALS

U.S. Marshals, Born and Bred

THE THIRD BOOK IN A SERIES ABOUT
A FAMILY OF U.S. MARSHALS, BY

Laura Marie Altom

HIS BABY BONUS
(#1110, April 2006)

U.S. Marshal Beauregard Logue has protected dozens
of witnesses, but none have affected him as deeply as
Ms. Gracie Sherwood. How this adorable—pregnant!—
blonde ended up the wife of a mobster, now a prison escapee,
he'll never know. Protecting Gracie until her ex-husband is
caught and sent to trial should be simple, right? Wrong!

Also available:
SAVING JOE
(#1086, October 2005)

MARRYING THE MARSHAL
(#1099, January 2006)

AND WATCH FOR ADAM'S STORY, COMING JULY 2006.

Available wherever Harlequin books are sold.
www.eHarlequin.com HARLAAPR